"Ah." Gabe straightened. "You made friends quickly. Willow's usually much more cautious in her dealings with strangers."

"She's a sweetie. You've done a great job of bringing her up. It can't have been easy for either of you—I mean, for a man to bring up a little girl, and for a little girl to grow up without her mother. Willow told me..." Caprice's voice trailed away as she saw Gabe stiffen.

His eyes had become hard, his lips tightly compressed. Caprice felt the air positively vibrate with tension. She had apparently said the wrong thing, but before she could even open her mouth to murmur sorry, he very pointedly—very rudely— tilted up his forearm and stared at his watch....

Grace Green grew up in Scotland, but later immigrated to Canada with her husband and children. They settled in "Beautiful Super Natural B.C." and Grace now lives in a house just minutes from ocean, beaches, mountains and rain forest. She makes no secret of her favorite occupation—her bumper sticker reads, I'd Rather Be Writing Romance! Grace also enjoys walking the seawall, gardening, getting together with other authors…and watching her characters come to life, because she knows that once they do, they will take over and write her stories for her.

Grace Green loves to write deeply emotional stories with compelling characters. She's also a great believer in creating happy-ever-after endings that are certain to bring a tear to your eye!

FOREVER WIFE AND MOTHER
Grace Green

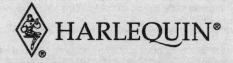

HARLEQUIN®

TORONTO • NEW YORK • LONDON
AMSTERDAM • PARIS • SYDNEY • HAMBURG
STOCKHOLM • ATHENS • TOKYO • MILAN • MADRID
PRAGUE • WARSAW • BUDAPEST • AUCKLAND

For Carolyn and Jan Willem

ISBN 0-373-03737-6

FOREVER WIFE AND MOTHER

First North American Publication 2003.

CHAPTER ONE

WHY had he lied to her?

Caprice Kincaid stood at the study window, tears misting her eyes as she watched three black limos sweep the last lingering mourners from Lockhart House. Never had she felt so lost, so alone…so bewildered. She had trusted her father all her life; it pained her heart now to know he had deceived her.

She *desperately* wanted to ask him why…but it was too late. He was gone. Forever gone. And she was left to wonder what deep dark secret he had been hiding—

"Excuse me, Mrs. Kincaid."

Blinking back her tears, she turned to see her father's lawyer, Michael Duggan, in the doorway.

"Michael." With a pale smile, she waved the bearded, heavyset man forward. "Thanks for waiting." The heels of her black pumps spiked into the plush bronze carpet as she crossed to her father's rosewood desk.

"You said you had something to show me."

Caprice slid open the desk's top drawer—the drawer she'd unlocked for the first time last night, with the tiny key she'd found in her father's wallet. Her fingers shook as she withdrew the sheet of age-yellowed paper—but she steadied them and quickly closed the drawer as the lawyer walked over to join her.

"As I told you the other day," he offered in a reassuring tone, "your father's will is straightforward. He

has left all his assets to you, as his only surviving rela-
tive. You are now one very wealthy young lady…."

Caprice handed him the paper. "This is my father's
birth certificate." A swath of her long ash-blond hair
slid over her cheek; abstractedly she looped it behind
her ear. "Dad always led me to believe he'd been born
in New York. Why would he have lied to me?"

The lawyer frowned. "According to this, he was born
in Washington State. That *is* a surprise!"

"To you, too?"

"Well, yeah…I had the impression he was born in
New York. I know that's where he met your mother—
and I know they moved here to Chicago before you were
born. But this place in Washington State…Hidden
Valley. Your father owns some riverside property
there—yours now, of course."

"What kind of property?"

"A log house. Modest place, with a bit of acreage."

"But his investments were all in apartment buildings,
weren't they?"

"Except for this house. Holly Cottage."

"Is it rented out?"

"Not at the moment, but over the past more than
twenty years your father donated it for the summer
months to a Seattle charity group called Break Away.
They used it as a retreat for women who for one reason
or another badly needed a holiday—a break—from problems in their lives."

"I had no idea…."

"After his second heart attack last fall, your father
indicated to Break Away that Holly Cottage would no
longer be available to them. He was planning to sell all
his holdings—and he did divest himself of all the apartment buildings—but he never got around to putting the

log house up for sale. Something seemed to be holding him back." He returned the birth certificate to Caprice. "I don't know what it was."

"I should like to find out."

"I'll make inquiries—"

"Thank you, Michael, but this is something I want to do myself. I'll come into the office on Monday to attend to the paperwork we discussed, and next day I'll fly out to Seattle. I've looked up Hidden Valley on the map—it's a couple of hours' drive from the city. I'll rent a car at the airport."

"You'll stay at Holly Cottage?"

"It'll be habitable?"

"Oh, sure, a caretaker looks after it."

"Then yes, I'll stay there."

"For how long?"

"For as long as it takes." Caprice's ebony silk blouse clung to her ribs as she drew in a deep breath. "Can you get me a key?"

"No problem. Come to think of it," the lawyer added as he prepared to leave, "it may not be a bad idea for you to take off for a while, have a vacation in the country. You've been under a lot of pressure over the past couple of years with your dad's failing health...."

Caprice waited till after Michael Duggan had gone before she opened the drawer again and withdrew the only other item she had found there: a photograph.

The snap was of a modest two-story log house, with a very lovely brunette posed at the front door.

On the back of the snap was written, in her father's strong familiar hand, just one word. Angela.

Caprice felt her heart twist as she looked at it. Her mother's name had been Kristin.

Who was she, this dark stranger who had been part

of her father's past? And why had he never talked about her?

It was a mystery.

And one she was determined to solve.

'Will! *Will!* Dammit, where *is* that girl?''

Willow Ryland woke with a start. Her father's voice, faint though it was, had penetrated her dreams. *Oh, cripes,* she thought frantically as she scrambled off the rocking chair where she'd dozed off, *I'm in big trouble if he finds me up here!*

She whipped off all the jewelry she'd bedecked herself with earlier—the silver charm bracelet, the ropes of pink pearls, the blue earrings, the gold brooch that spelled out Angela—and tucked them away swiftly in the bottom of the old trunk, under the silk dresses and scarves and straw hats and wonderfully shiny high-heeled sandals, before lowering the lid carefully so as not to make any noise.

''Will! Where are you and that damned dog?''

At the word *dog,* Fang stirred and gave a protesting growl. He'd been dozing, too, his squat little body stretched out on the planked floor in a beam of April sunshine that slanted through the attic skylight.

''Hush!'' Willow hissed as she clambered onto the rickety table that sat below the skylight. Raising herself on her toes, she peered out. And—oh, cripes!—there he was, striding around the car park, looking every which way. For her. Then all at once he turned on his heel and strode toward the lodge. His face, she noticed, was set in a dark scowl.

''Oh, hell!'' The bad word popped out before she could stop it. She'd have to say an extra prayer that night. ''Fang, let's get out of here!''

The black and white mongrel's claws clicked as he scurried across the floor and then lolloped down the narrow winding stairs that led to the third floor. Willow climbed down after him backward, rolling her eyes as the dog lost his footing and his roly-poly body landed with a fat thud against the door at the bottom of the steps.

Cautiously, she opened the door a crack. She heard nothing. She crept out, with Fang rudely pushing ahead, and closed the door again. She turned the key in the lock, and biting her lip, planted the key where she'd first found it a year ago, in the shadowy cranny of a glass-doored bookcase, across from one of the guest bedrooms.

Then—heart thumping like mad—she sped to the passage and the landing.

Fang was already halfway down to the second floor. And when she caught up with him, she gulped at the sight of her father in the foyer. He was scratching a hand through his wavy black hair and muttering to himself.

"Dad!" she called. "Hi!"

He raised his head sharply, and she saw relief flood his eyes before sparks of irritation sent it flying.

"Where the hell have you been?" he asked. "I've been looking everywhere for—"

"Dad." She used the same tone Miss Atkinson had used last week when the teacher had sent her to the principal's office for wrestling with her best friend Mark at recess. "You're not allowed to say hell. Remember?"

She saw his lips twitch. "Right. Sorry, Will. I'll try to do better."

Willow grabbed the banister, swung her leg over and swooped down with her back to him. He caught her— as she'd known he would—just as she shot off the end.

"So...where were you?" he said gruffly as he set her down. "You and that stupid mutt of yours?"

"Oh, just busy," she said, cocking her head at him. And just loving him, like she always did. "Were you calling me? I didn't hear you. What did you want?"

"Dinner's ready," he said. "Bacon burgers."

Her very favorite dinner!

Happily, she skipped alongside him as they made their way along the passage leading to their private quarters, to the cozy little kitchen—which was her favorite room in the lodge, second only to the attic.

And this was her favorite time of year. The ski season was over, the summer season hadn't started, the staff were on holiday, so she had her dad all to herself. Things would be different in two weeks when the lodge would be jam-packed with guests...and then he'd be off into the wilderness with a bunch of rich folks who wanted to do all that neat stuff like rock climbing and white-water rafting.

For now, she wanted to enjoy being alone with her dad. Who was the best dad in the world.

She'd eaten two bacon burgers, washed down with milk, before she noticed something that turned her blood cold.

She'd forgotten to take off the wedding ring.

It glowed like a firefly on her middle finger—the only finger it fit. And it was a miracle, truly a miracle, that he hadn't noticed it yet.

Palms sweating, she snuck her hands under the table, slid off the gold band and poked it down deep into the side pocket of her overalls. Only when it was safely tucked away did she dare glance at him again.

But he was lost in thought. She could tell by the lonesome look in his eyes, the look that told her he was aching for something. She had never figured out what. It reminded her, though, of the way she looked when she chanced to see herself in a mirror when she was thinking that it was the saddest thing in the whole world not to have a mom and how she longed with all her heart to have one.

At any rate, her dad hadn't noticed the ring. And for that, she was truly grateful. He had no idea that she spent time in the attic—she knew for a fact that he never went up there himself. First time she went up, the floor and every other thing had been inches deep in dust, and it had taken her two full weeks to get everything cleaned off.

And of course he had no idea she had found the trunk of pretty things. He had no idea that she loved jewelry and silk dresses and shiny shoes and straw hats with pink flowers. He didn't. He didn't like pretty things.

And he didn't like pretty ladies.

She knew that for a fact!

And it was why, from the very moment she'd overheard him say it—when she was four years old, which was three years ago now—she'd known that if he was gonna love her she had to make herself look as ugly as a mud road.

And actually, she reflected as she considered her raggedy straw-yellow hair, her turned-up nose and her too-big eyes that weren't even the same color as each other—that wasn't a very hard thing to do!

Heck, no, she thought with a grin, it wasn't hard at all.

In fact, it was a downright cinch!

'Hidden Valley?'' Peering into the murky night, the gas jockey indicated a road across the highway from the rural Shell station. "Go straight down there for a couple of miles and you'll come to a village, go through it and on up the valley for another ten miles. The Lockhart place ain't signposted but look for the Ryland's Resort sign—you can't miss it, it's well lit up. Your turnoff's right after."

Caprice had no problem following the directions, but the drive from Seattle had taken longer than she'd expected, so it was almost midnight before she finally saw the illuminated Ryland's Resort sign.

Slowing down, she passed the entrance to the private road, and sixty yards farther on came to her turnoff.

As she swung onto the track, the headlights of her rented Honda danced among the pine trees lining the trail. She drove cautiously and in a minute rounded a bend and entered a clearing. The log house lay straight ahead.

She drew the Honda to a halt by the gate of a picket fence that enclosed a good-size garden and sat there a while, rubbing her neck to iron out the knots. Then she slung the strap of her purse over her shoulder, hauled her overnight bag from the seat beside her, flicked the lights off and eased her travel-weary body out of the car.

Momentarily blinded by the dark, she paused to let her eyes adjust and felt the night enfold her.

The air was rich with the scent of evergreens and musky with the odor of damp earth. Deep in the forest, a creature howled, and as the sound echoed eerily from the hills, Caprice shivered. She became suddenly aware of how alone she was here, alone and unprotected.

Stirring herself, she picked her way along the path to the door and dropped her overnight bag at the side of the porch before taking the key from her purse. It turned easily in the lock, and she pushed the door forward.

The entryway was tar dark. Leaving the door open, she ran a hand over the wall in search of a light switch, but as she groped for it something brushed past her from inside with a cry so harsh and high it chilled her blood.

She froze for one long, terrified moment. And then, with panic racing at her heels, she ran helter-skelter to the car and flung herself breathlessly inside.

Fang heard it first.

Gabe was waiting at the top of the lodge steps for the mutt to do his bedtime business and emerge from the forest when the animal gave a sharp warning bark.

As the sound faded, Gabe heard the throb of a fast-approaching engine. Seconds later, he saw the glare of headlights, and a car roared into the clearing.

Tensing, he drew his hands from the pockets of his jeans. Strangers in the night. Nowadays, one couldn't be too careful.

As the car slammed to a skidding halt a few yards from the lodge steps, Fang rocketed over to the vehicle, barking wildly while dancing around it in a frenzy of excitement.

"Fang!" Gabe yelled. "Come here!"

Still yelping shrilly, the dog obeyed, hopping up the steps to take his stance beside his master.

Gabe snapped his fingers. "Quiet!"

After a low protesting growl, Fang became silent.

The powerful light above the lodge's entrance beamed onto the car. It was a Honda Civic, and only one person was in it. Warily, Gabe watched the driver climb out and felt his tension ease when he saw the intruder was a female—a slight, petite figure in jeans and a dark shirt. The woman paused, her hands cupped at her brow to shield her eyes from the light, and then walked hesitantly forward.

She stopped at the foot of the stairs, and with her face shadowed by her hands, she looked at him.

"I know it's late," she said. "But can you give me a room for the night?"

"Sorry." Her hair, he saw, was fair—and wildly disheveled, which struck him as odd, because there wasn't even the slightest breeze. But maybe the storm-swept look was in...along with the black feathers adorning her tousled coiffure. As far as he was concerned, whichever designer had decreed feathers-in-the-hair this season had to be cuckoo himself. "Didn't you read the sign on the highway? We're not open for another couple of weeks."

"Oh, dear." She gave a shaky sigh. "Where's the nearest motel?"

"Your best bet's Cedarville. That's about an hour's drive—"

He broke off as she swayed.

He frowned. "You okay?"

No response. She stood there, looking dazed and boneless as a puppet. And then she crumpled.

Good grief! He lunged down the steps and caught her just before she hit the gravel.

Sweeping her up in his arms, he glowered at her—at her feather-strewn hair, her closed eyelids, her face—which was deathly pale except for a few dirty smears.

"Hey," he growled, giving her a brisk shake. "Wake up. You can't sleep here. We're closed!"

No response.

He hesitated and dithered and swithered and then finally wheeled around and carted the stranger up the steps, all the while muttering words under his breath that he'd never have used in front of Will.

As he went inside, Fang took off for their private quarters to sleep in Will's room, as he always did.

Kicking the door shut with his heel, Gabe walked across the foyer and into the public lounge. He flicked on a light, crossed to the nearest sofa and deposited the woman on it.

Then he crossed to the bar and poured a tot of brandy into a glass before returning to the sofa. He tilted the stranger's head, poured a little brandy into her mouth. She swallowed, coughed, choked and then with a sputter shook her head and slowly raised her eyelids.

She looked at him. Her eyes were wide-spaced, long-lashed and smoky gray. They had a blank expression.

"What happened?" she asked, her voice husky.

"You passed out."

She blinked. "I did? Where?"

"At the lodge's front entrance."

She looked blank for a few seconds longer, and then she said, "Ah, I remember now." Her lips twisted in a wry smile. "I guess I don't react well to rejection!"

"It's to be hoped you aren't faced with it too often," he said dryly. "Falling down can be hazardous to your health."

"Thanks," she said. "But I'm fine now."

She didn't look fine. She looked all in. And not merely tired. There was a bone-deep weariness about her and an aching sadness in her eyes that—if she had been a part of his life—would have worried him. Well, she wasn't a part of his life, so he needn't spend one second fretting about her. In fact, the sooner he got rid of her the better.

She struggled to a sitting position. "I'm sorry to be such a bother." Dragging a hand through her hair, she dislodged one of the black feathers, and it clung to her knuckles. When she saw it, she flicked it off with a shocked sound. Horrified, she said, "Where did *that* come from?" It fluttered to the carpet.

Gabe plucked it up and got to his feet. "From your hair. Don't worry, the others are still there."

"The others?" Lurching off the sofa, she flicked her fingers frantically through her hair. He noticed the gleam of a gold wedding band on her ring finger. "Where?"

"Stand still." So the feathers weren't a fashion statement. Then where the dickens had they come from? He picked out the remaining few feathers. "There." He held them in his palm. "All present and accounted for."

She made a grimace of distaste.

He strolled to the hearth and let the feathers drift into a trash can. As he brushed his fingers together, he heard her murmur something that sounded like, "Must have been a bird."

"Mmm?" He turned, eyebrows raised.

"Oh, nothing. Thank you for the brandy, but I'd better be getting along now. Could you give me directions to Cedarville? And if you know the name of a motel there, perhaps you could let me use your phone so I can call ahead."

He opened his mouth to say, sure, she could use his phone. And then he shut it again. This woman was in no condition to drive. It would be on his head if he let her go and she passed out again and ended up in the river.

He heaved out an *I can't believe I'm doing this* sigh and said, "You can stay here tonight."

Her gray eyes widened, and she stared at him as if she couldn't believe it, either. Then she smiled, a smile that lit up her grimy face and made her look like an apprentice chimney sweep who'd been given the day off.

"Really? Oh, I *do* appreciate your kindness." She offered her right hand and said, somewhat shyly, "I'm Caprice Kincaid."

"Gabe Ryland." Her fingers were fine-boned, the skin incredibly smooth. "At your service. So, Mrs. Kincaid, do you have an overnight bag?"

"Yes, it's in the—oh!" She stopped short, looking embarrassed. "I, um, no, I have a case—it's in the trunk. I'll go out for it—"

"I'll get it."

"Oh. Thanks. You'll find my key in the ignition. Could you bring in my purse, too, please? I left it on the passenger seat."

"Will do."

When he came back, she was looking at his wall of framed photos adjacent to the bar—photographs he'd taken over the years, candid shots of his well-heeled guests on the mountains, on the river, in the wilderness.

She turned to him. "What kind of resort do you run? It's obviously not geared to couch potatoes!"

"I run a ski school in winter, and in summer I take parties white-water rafting, rock climbing, that sort of thing. Outward Bound," he added with a sardonic smile, "meets 'Lifestyles of the Rich and Famous.'"

"So you're in-between times at present?"

"Yeah. We open again in May." He led her out of the lounge and to the stairs, where he paused. Indicating a passage to his left, he said, "Our private quarters are through there, but I'll put you on the first floor. All the guest rooms have en suite bathrooms. You should find everything you need. If you don't—" he shrugged and looked at her over his shoulder as he ascended the stairs ahead of her "—you'll have to make do." He yawned. "I'm going to bed myself now."

At the top of the stairs he turned right and opened the door to the first room he came to. It was Spartan, as all the guests' rooms were, except for the bed, which was luxuriously comfortable.

He laid her case on the luggage rack. And then crossed to the window. He paused, his long fingers curled around the edge of the heavy cotton drapes, and looked over the valley. The night was dark, but he could see dots of light marking the houses and farms farther up the river.

His gaze hardened as he fixed it on the spot where he knew the Lockhart place to be. There he could see nothing. No pinpoint, no spark of light. But any day now, as sure as the sun would rise tomorrow morning, the first of Malcolm Lockhart's charity cases would be turning up at Holly Cottage. Some woman from the city, who would spend a couple of weeks recuperating from whatever trauma had brought her there. As soon as she left, another would arrive. And so it would go on, till after the autumn leaves had turned and winter came again to the valley.

If his gaze was hard, his heart was even harder. The Lockhart place should, by rights, belong to him. Just as it should have belonged to his father, and his father's father before him. His father's hatred of Malcolm Lockhart was matched only by his own. And it was a hatred that would stay with him till his dying day.

"Mr. Ryland?"

He closed the drapes brusquely before turning. Mrs. Kincaid was looking at him with a concerned expression.

"Are you all right?" she asked. "I said your name several times and you...didn't seem to hear."

"My mind drifted for a moment." He strode to the bathroom door and swung it open. Everything was as it should be—spick-and-span, with fresh white towels, a basket of basic toiletries, clean glasses, a bottle of Evian.

"Breakfast's at seven. Sharp!" He started toward the bedroom door. "I hope you'll find the room comfortable."

"It's lovely," she said. "I can't tell you how grateful I am. Oh, one thing before you go…"

He turned at the door, his eyebrows raised.

"Will it disturb anyone if I have a shower? I've been traveling since dawn…. I'd really like to get cleaned up."

"No problem. You won't disturb me, I sleep like a log. And as for Will—you could drop a bomb next to the bed and you wouldn't wake her."

As he walked to the landing, he felt a pang of guilt. Seven o'clock was an early start for somebody as utterly exhausted as this young woman obviously was.

But he staved off the guilty twinges by reminding himself that if he hadn't taken her in, she'd still be on the road.

And if she couldn't manage to haul her skinny little body out of bed by seven, then she'd just have to go hungry!

CHAPTER TWO

CAPRICE woke next morning to the sound of a dog's bark.

The bedroom was in darkness. She reached for her watch, peered at the luminous hands and saw that it was six-thirty. Lying back, she let her mind drift over the events of last night and grimaced as she recalled her panicky flight from Holly Cottage, scared out of her wits by nothing more than a bird—a crow?—that had tumbled down the sitting-room chimney!

She'd been appalled when she'd seen her reflection in the mirror. With her tangled hair and soot-smudged face, she'd looked like a street urchin. It was a wonder Gabe Ryland had let her through his doorway.

Gabe Ryland.

How different he was from the men in her social circle with their city suits and their *GQ* coiffures—men with pale smooth hands and smoother moves. Gabe Ryland was rugged and weather-beaten, with a hard, craggy face and black hair that hadn't been cut in months. And in his sturdy jeans, hiking boots and no-nonsense plaid shirt, he'd been a walking ad for his Outward Bound business.

His hands, she remembered, were rough.

And his manners, she remembered, were rougher.

"You should find everything you need," he'd said, and added bluntly, "if you don't...you'll have to make do." Talk about uncompromising! And then, "Breakfast's at seven sharp,'' the implication being that if she turned up at one minute past, she'd have to go hungry.

And, she mused over a wide yawn, she *was* hungry.

She got up and padded to the window.

When she pulled back the drapes, she saw that dawn was just breaking. The eastern sky was bloodshot, and rosy light was creeping along the green valley and painting the unruffled surface of the river a glorious shade of pink.

It was going to be a perfect day.

And she just had time, she decided with a lilt of anticipation, to squeeze in a quick walk before breakfast.

''Fang, come *here!*''

Fang scrambled through a clump of ferns, and as he bumped against Will's legs, she caught him by the collar. ''Hush!'' she whispered urgently. ''Someone's coming!''

She held her breath as she peeked out from behind the trunk of the oak tree, which was just a few yards from the fence. Cripes, if it was her dad she'd be in deep trouble. She wasn't supposed to be on Lockhart land; he'd kill her if he knew she'd set foot on it.

He'd warned her *never* to cross the fence, warned her when she first became old enough to play outside alone.

''Why, Dad?'' she'd asked, as they stood on their grassy slope and looked over the fence at the strip of forest that lay between the fence and the river.

''You don't need to know why,'' he'd told her. ''Just remember, no trespassing on Lockhart land.''

And she'd obeyed him. For a whole month she'd done as he'd told her. But then one June evening Fang had taken off under the barbed wire fence chasing after a rabbit...and he hadn't come back. There was a wooden

stile close to the spot where he'd wriggled under. She'd
perched on the top slat and waited. And waited. And
waited. Not knowing what to do. And worried sick about
him.

In the end, she'd gone in.

Just across the fence was a path into the forest, and
she'd followed it, calling for Fang as she went. The path
had soon led her to a log house, and in the garden she'd
found Fang. But he wasn't alone. He was with a lady.
And the lady was petting him and cuddling him...and
crying.

Will was happy to see Fang safe and sound but sad
to see the lady cry. She went into the garden and told
the lady who she was. She and the lady talked, and the
lady—whose name was Emily—told her some secrets.
When the sun went down, Emily walked through the
trees with her as far as the wooden stile.

After that, Will took Fang to Holly Cottage as often
as she could, but only between May and October and
only when her dad was away. This was the first time
ever that she'd risked going onto Lockhart land while
he was home, and she really didn't know what had
brought her there today.

She hadn't gone as far as the log house, though, because the Lockhart summer ladies didn't start coming
till the first of May, but she'd climbed over the stile and
skipped down the forest path a bit with Fang.

And was on her way back for breakfast—was close
enough to the stile to see it through the trees—when
she'd heard someone up ahead.

Holding her breath, she peeked around the trunk of
the oak tree. And her heart almost stopped when she saw
a stranger on the other side of the fence, standing with
one hand atop a fence post.

Fang barked.

Will got such a start she lost her grip on his collar, and he lurched from their hiding place and bounded to the fence.

Tail whisking like mad, he yelped ferociously at the stranger. She stepped back. Which made him bark even louder. On and on and on…

There was nothing for it, Will thought, frustrated, but to come out. If she didn't, her dad might hear Fang and come to investigate.

So she put on her scowliest face and marched out of the shadows. Grabbing Fang's collar, she ordered him to hush. Which he did. Then she held up the bottom wire and pushed him under the fence before climbing over the stile to the other side.

By the time she'd clambered over, the stranger had crouched down and was making friends with Fang, whose tail might well drop off, Will thought disapprovingly, if he kept wagging it that fast!

She frowned at the stranger, who wasn't very big. And she was *real* skinny. She had blond hair that was scooped up in a high ponytail but would probably reach halfway down her back if it wasn't. Her white T-shirt was tucked into her blue jeans, and she was wearing white Reeboks. Will had just finished giving her a good once-over when the woman stood up and fixed smiley gray eyes on her.

"Hi," she said. "What a dear little dog."

Will folded her arms over her chest and said, in a growly voice, "You're trespassing. This is Ryland property. You'd best get off it real fast, before my dad catches you."

The stranger looked past Will, across the fence. "I was just wondering," she said, "where that path leads."

"You can't go down there, either. That property belongs to old man Lockhart—" Will stopped abruptly as her watch beeped an alarm. "Cripes," she muttered. "It's seven. If I want breakfast I'd better—" Dodging around the stranger and saying, "C'mon, Fang!" she hurtled away up the hill, not breaking her stride as she called over her shoulder, "Like I said, lady, you'd best get going real fast or you'll be staring up the barrel of my dad's shotgun!"

Caprice chuckled.

And started up the slope.

A tomboy, she mused as the child disappeared over the crest of the hill, but an adorable one, with that raggedy yellow hair, delightfully tip-tilted nose and lovely eyes. Mismatched eyes, one green, one hazel, and densely fringed with lashes the color of toffee.

Caprice paused and looked back when she reached the top of the slope. Over the tips of the trees, she could see three chimney pots. If that was Lockhart land, then that would be the log house. Holly Cottage.

What secrets might she uncover there? Would she find some clue as to why her father had deceived her? If not, she'd have to become acquainted with the locals in the hopes of finding someone who'd known him and would talk about him. Under the circumstances, it would be unwise to ask anyone outright if Malcolm Lockhart had been involved with a woman called Angela. Who knew what can of worms that might open up! No, better to play it safe, be discreet.

Heaving a restless sigh, she turned and walked on. At the lodge, she went in by the main entrance. She was hesitating in the foyer, unsure where to go, when the little girl shot out from the passage leading to the Rylands' private quarters.

She skidded to a halt when she saw Caprice.

"Are you Mrs. Kincaid?" Her whisper was panicky.

"Yes."

The child gulped. "Mrs. Kincaid, please don't tell my dad you saw me on the other side of the fence. That's Lockhart property and…" Her cheeks took on a guilty flush. "*I* was the one who was trespassing. Not you." Taking a deep breath, she added in a rush, "I'm not supposed to go in there. If my dad found out, he'd be as mad as—"

"It's okay," Caprice assured her. "Your secret's safe with me."

"Oh, thank you—"

"Will!" Gabe Ryland's voice thundered from somewhere in the depths of the lodge. "Did you find her?"

Caprice raised her eyebrows. "You're Will?"

"Yup."

"Oh, I thought when your father spoke of Will last night he was referring to…your mother."

The child's eyes became shuttered. "My mother's dead," she said. "It's been just me and my dad since I was four."

"Oh, I'm so sorry—"

"Will!"

At the sound of her father's bellow, the little girl said, "Uh-oh! We'd better get into the kitchen if we want to eat. C'mon!"

She darted off, and Caprice followed her to the kitchen, which turned out to be small and cozy and bright, with windows facing east. The sun beamed in and cast its pink glow over a jade-green slate floor, granite countertops, maple cupboards and a maple island.

Fang was in a corner of the room, digging his nose greedily into a bowl of dog food, and Gabe Ryland was standing with his back to her at a round maple table set in a windowed alcove. He was wearing khaki shorts and a khaki shirt, and she found her gaze flicking in awe over his wide shoulders, his lean hips, his long, brawny legs. Talk about rugged! Talk about tough! Talk about powerful! She could well imagine this man leaping mountains in a single bound or overpowering a cougar with one twist of his bare hands.

He said to Will as she clambered onto her chair, "Did you find Mrs. Kincaid?"

"She did," Caprice said.

He turned around, a coffee carafe in his hand. "Oh, hi, there."

"Good morning," Caprice murmured, adding with an edge of humour in her voice, "I hope I'm not late?"

"Rules," he said, "are meant to be kept." Amusement gleamed in his eyes—hunter green eyes that were so intense Caprice could almost feel them lasering into her soul. He glanced at his daughter. "Right, Will?"

The child wriggled uncomfortably in her chair, and to save her from being put on the spot, Caprice interjected lightly, "Some say that rules are for the obedience of fools and the guidance of idiots."

"Without rules," he returned as he poured coffee into two mugs, "the world would be an even crazier place than it already is."

Caprice took the seat he indicated. "But surely there are times when we must break the rules—"

"It may be more difficult, at those times, to keep to them, but in the long run it works out for the best. As long as the rule is a good one to start with." He returned the carafe to the coffeemaker and brought a rack of toast to the table. "Take mealtimes. If the rule is that we always sit down at a certain time and we all adhere to that rule, it makes the cook's work easier." His eyes teased her. "Don't you think so?"

"What I *think*—" Caprice added milk to her coffee "—is that it's far too early in the day for such a discussion."

"Mrs. Kincaid's right, Dad." Will looked up from her bowl of cereal. "It's far too early."

"Outnumbered." He held up his palms in surrender, and smiled.

He had a devastating smile. Wide, warm, sincere. A generous flash of blindingly white teeth, a merry twinkle of laughing green eyes, an irresistibly seductive charisma.

Caprice felt her pulse scatter in wild disarray and she struggled to get it back to its regular rhythm. Wherever this man went, she decided dazedly, he must surely leave a trail of broken hearts behind.

He rested his hands on his hips. "Mrs. Kincaid—"

She forced herself to pay attention. "It's Caprice."

"Caprice. What can I offer you? Bacon and eggs? Sausage, tomatoes, mushrooms, hash browns?"

"Thanks, but I don't eat a cooked breakfast."

"Lucky for you!" Will sputtered over a mouthful of her cereal. "'Cause Dad can't cook worth a—well, he just can't cook! Coffee and bacon burgers are his specialties—and toast—but he even sometimes burns the toast!" She giggled as her father put on a highly indignant expression.

"Young lady!" He waved a teaspoon at her. "You'd better remember which side your bread is buttered on or you'll be sent off to boarding school—"

He broke off as the phone rang. Excusing himself, he crossed the room to answer it.

As he talked to someone, Will said confidently, "Don't worry, Mrs. Kincaid, my dad would never send me away. He'd miss me too much. Also," she whispered confidingly, "he couldn't possibly send me to boarding school. We couldn't afford it. He's been saving every spare penny for years to buy a piece of riverfront property...if one should ever come up for sale. Which it doesn't look like it's ever gonna," she finished in a rush as her father put down the phone. She looked up, all wide-eyed and innocent, as he returned to the table.

He sat across from Caprice. "That was Mark's mother, Will. She can't drive you and Mark to school today. I told her I'll do it." He shifted his attention to Caprice. "So once you've had breakfast and got your things organized, I'll see you on your way. I'll have to lock up here before I take off to pick up Mark. He lives quite a way from here."

"Of course."

Caprice was surprised to find herself reluctant to leave. Half an hour ago, she'd been feeling restless, impatient to get to Holly Cottage. But Gabe Ryland was a very intriguing man, and his daughter was delightful, and she was drawn to stay longer. Drawn to get to know them better.

But that would be foolish, she mused as she nibbled a corner of her toast. She had come to the valley to get some answers, and as soon as she got them she'd be gone. There was no point in getting emotionally involved with any of the inhabitants. No point at all.

"Tell me, Mr. Ryland," she said, "how many staff do you employ here?"

"It's Gabe. Staff? Half a dozen, give or take. The

same people have been coming for the past several years. The housekeeper—"

"That's Mrs. Malone!" Will said.

"—and a cook—"

"That's Mrs. Carter, who also looks after me when Dad's away."

"—a housemaid and a waitress—"

"Jane and Patsy." Will finished her glass of milk.

Gabe grinned at her. "An odd job man—"

"Sandy McIntosh." Will set down the glass and swiped a paper serviette over her mouth. "He drives me to school when Dad's away—well, he takes turns with Mark's mom."

"—and Alex Tremaine—"

"He's my dad's best guide and instructor, Mrs. Kincaid. He teaches people how to do rock climbing and mountaineering and canoeing and backpacking, and most of all, how to do white water, and like my dad he teaches people who go on the white-water expeditions. They learn how to read the river and how to paddle and how to be safe. I just can't wait," she added eagerly, "for next summer. My dad's going to take me hiking in the wilderness for the first time. I'll be nine by then. How old are you, Mrs. Kincaid?"

"Will," her father chided her gently, "you know better than to ask a lady her age!"

Will grimaced. "Sorry, Mrs. Kincaid, I didn't mean to be rude."

"No problem." Caprice smiled as she gathered her dishes. "I'm going to be twenty-seven in June."

"Dad's eight years older than you are. And his birthday's on the fourth of July. He always makes sure he's home that day, and we have a gi-normous party, with fireworks."

"Will." Her father rose from the table. "If you're finished, you should go to the guest lounge and—"

"Practice my piano." Rolling her eyes, the child got up and carted her dishes to the counter. "I know, Dad." She turned to Caprice. "Goodbye, Mrs. Kincaid, it's been truly nice meeting you. And thanks for…you know."

"My pleasure," Caprice said.

As the child left, Caprice rose and carried her dishes to the counter.

"What was that all about?" Gabe bent over and slotted the dishes into the dishwasher.

"Oh, just girl stuff."

"Ah." He straightened. "You made friends quickly. Will's usually much more cautious in her dealings with strangers."

"She's a sweetie. You've done a great job of bringing her up. It can't have been easy for either of you—I mean, for a man to bring up a little girl, and for a little girl to grow up without her mother. Will told me…." Her voice trailed away as she saw him stiffen.

His eyes had become hard, his lips tightly compressed. She felt the air vibrate with tension. She had apparently said the wrong thing, but before she could even open her mouth to murmur sorry, he very pointedly—very rudely!—tilted his forearm and stared at his watch.

Caprice felt her cheeks grow scarlet, partly from embarrassment but more from indignation. "I'll go now," she said stiltedly, "and gather my things together. Then I'll settle my bill and be off."

"There's no charge."

"But—"

"It'll only screw up my bookkeeping."

His curt, dismissive tone riled her. She wasn't used to

being spoken to like that, and she didn't like it. And now she didn't like him, either!

But she was still a guest at his lodge.

Biting back a stinging retort, she spun on her heel and stalked from the kitchen.

She felt his cold gaze follow her but she'd gone only a few yards along the passage when she heard a frustrated, "Damn!" followed by the loud thump of a clenched fist being smashed against the wall or the countertop.

She raised her eyebrows. Temper, temper!

She was still wondering whether he was angry with her or himself when she reached the foot of the stairs and heard the sound of piano music coming from the lounge. Her mouth twisted in an ironic smile. Will was practicing.

And the piece the child had chosen was "Home Sweet Home."

"Dad, where was Mrs. Kincaid going after she left the lodge?"

"I didn't ask." Gabe turned his Range Rover off the highway and up the Hoopers' farm road.

"Where did she come from?"

"I don't know. Why the interest?"

Will hugged her lunch bucket to her chest. "I'm worried about her. She looked sad."

"Honey, the world is full of sad people. You can't worry about all of them."

"I don't."

He turned his head briefly and found she was looking at him with a grave expression. "But you're worried about Mrs. Kincaid?"

She nodded.

He turned his attention to the road again. They approached the farm gate. "Well, don't. You'll never see her again, and anyway, worrying never did any good. It only burns up energy."

"It's a pity she doesn't have a dog."

Gabe felt a flash of amusement. "You think?"

"Oh, yes. Dogs make people happy."

"Dogs are a lot of work." He saw Mark running from the rambling old farmhouse to the gate. "They have to be fed and watered and walked and cleaned up after."

"I'm not talking about the work part of it." He felt her earnest gaze on him. "I'm talking about the feel-good part. When a person hugs a dog and strokes it and looks into its eyes, and the dog looks back and licks your hand and just be's a friend…that's what makes people happy." He noticed she was so caught up in what she was saying, for once she didn't wave to Mark. "I saw a program on TV one time and it said that having a dog around makes old people feel better, so I figured if it makes old people feel better it should work on sad people, too. And know what? It does."

Gabe had been listening with only half a mind, but something in the intensity of her tone snapped him to full attention.

Pulling the vehicle to a halt by the gate, he turned in his seat and looked at her. She was staring into space.

"Will?"

She didn't seem to hear.

He waved a hand in front of her face. "Honey, how do you know?"

Blinking, she looked at him. "Know what?"

"That dogs make sad people happy?"

"Oh, that." She swallowed. "No reason. I just—"

Mark wrenched open the Range Rover's back door

and clambered in. With a cheery greeting—"Hi, Will,
hi, Mr. Ryland, thanks for picking me up"—he set his
lunch bucket at his feet and fastened his seat belt.

Gabe put the vehicle in motion. "Hi, kid."

Mark immediately launched into a tale about one of
his father's cows that had calved the previous evening,
and Gabe knew his opportunity to question his daughter
was lost.

But he couldn't dismiss the feeling that something
was going on, something he knew nothing about...and
she obviously meant to keep it that way.

And Mrs. Kincaid's sadness—which he himself had
noticed—was what had brought it to the surface.

Well, neither he nor his daughter would be seeing the
woman again, so they could both forget about her.

He dropped the kids off at school and drove home.
Once there, he fetched Fang from the kitchen and took
him out for a run. The day was polished to a bright
sheen, the sky as blue as sapphire, with not one cloud
to mar it.

He strolled down the grassy slope in front of the
lodge, over the crest and down the hill. Fang romped
ahead, making for the barbed wire fence that formed the
boundary between Ryland property and Lockhart land.
Gabe shook his head irritably as, just like every other
morning, the dog made to wriggle under the lowest wire
of the fence.

"Fang!" he yelled. "No!"

The dog paused halfway through. Then, just as he did
every morning on their walk, he wriggled back and took
off along the perimeter.

Damn dog! Gabe mused. *You'd think he'd know by
now that he wasn't supposed to go in there.*

His lips compressed to a thin line as he gazed over

the forest, the only evidence of Holly Cottage being the
three chimney tops—

But no. Not this morning.

This morning, marring the clear blue of the sky, a
wisp of smoke rose from one of the chimneys; rose, and
swayed in a gust of wind off the river, and rose again.

Gabe rammed his hands into his pockets and glowered
at the smoke. As a child, he'd been ordered never to
trespass on Lockhart land, but once, when he was seven,
he'd dared to sneak down there, and he'd peeked in the
kitchen window. He'd seen an old wood stove in the
shadowy room, and he'd always remembered it because
it had been so old-fashioned compared to the modern
appliances they had at the lodge.

He imagined someone in that kitchen, a young woman
from the city who would be lighting that stove every
day.

And though he knew he was sending hostile vibes to
the wrong person, he couldn't help wishing that whoever
had set that fire would vanish off the face of the earth,
because any sign of life from the old log house was
a reminder of something—and someone—he dearly
wished to forget.

CHAPTER THREE

CAPRICE felt a sudden shiver ice her skin.

Which was odd, she mused, since the kitchen was so toasty warm with the wood fire roaring in the stove. What was it people said about those involuntary shudders? Someone stepping over your grave...

But she didn't want to think about graves. It was only a week since she'd stood at her father's, and losing him was almost more than she could bear. At least having the Angela mystery to solve would keep her busy—give her a goal.

But where to start?

It was too bad she'd rubbed Gabe Ryland the wrong way before she'd asked any questions about her father. She'd have to put out feelers elsewhere. Perhaps the best place to start would be the village she'd passed through last night. It was only ten minutes away.

She wouldn't go till later, though; she was bushed. Closing her eyes, she leaned back in the cushioned walnut rocking chair and let her thoughts roam to her arrival at Holly Cottage that morning.

She'd been relieved to find her overnight bag on the porch where she'd abandoned it, but her relief had soon turned to frustration when she'd gone into the cottage and found the mess wrought by the panic-stricken bird.

It had taken her all morning to clean up. The only godsend had been that the caretaker had set the wood stove, so all she'd had to do was put a match to it. By the time she'd finished her scrubbing and mopping and was ready for lunch, the kitchen had been warm as pie.

Now, after a second cup of milky tea, she was not only bushed, she was sleepy. She'd doze for half an hour, she decided with a yawn, then she'd drive to the village and get her investigation under way.

"Thanks, Janet." Gabe took his mail from the postmistress and started to turn away. "See you tomorrow."

"Hang on, Angel."

Gabe rolled his eyes. As a child, everyone had called him by his given name, Gabriel, but everyone called him Gabe now...except for Janet Black, who still referred to him by the nickname she'd given him when he was a toddler. And the words "Hang on, Angel!" usually indicated that she had a choice piece of gossip to pass on. "I'm in a bit of a rush today, Janet—"

"You'll want to hear this." The woman planted her sharp elbows on the counter and leaned forward confidentially. "We have a stranger in our midst!"

"The first of many, Janet. The tourist season's getting under way and—"

"This one—" Janet threw a furtive glance toward the farthest aisle "—has been asking questions."

Casually, Gabe looked around but could see no one. "About what?"

"About Malcolm Lockhart."

Gabe turned slowly to the postmistress. "What kind of questions?"

The postmistress's eyes gleamed with satisfaction. "I knew that'd get your attention." Keeping her voice low, she said, "She asked how long I'd lived in the valley. And I thought she was just being chatty so I told her. 'Born and brought up here,' said I. 'And been postmistress for the past thirty years.' 'Oh,' sez she, 'I guess you'll know just about everybody in the area then.'''

"And you said…"

"And I said, 'Better than most folks. You can tell a lot about people by the mail they get!' She laughed at that, and then she said, all airy-fairy-like, 'Can you tell me anything about a man called Malcolm Lockhart—I believe he used to live at Holly Cottage, on the river?' And the minute she said Malcolm Lockhart, my ears went on red alert. Well, Angel, we all know *that* story…and the first thing I think of is, is she a reporter? Has she come to poke around and do a write-up? After all, it's coming up to thirty years since the scandal and—"

"What else—" Gabe's voice was harsh "—did she ask?"

"That was it. As soon as I figured she was snooping, I closed up tighter than a bank on Sunday!" The post-mistress sucked in a sharp breath. "There she is now!" She nodded urgently toward the front checkout. "She's just leaving. Do you know her, Angel? You ever seen her before?"

Gabe followed her gaze…and felt his chest tighten. Oh, yes, he knew her. He knew her, all right. She had spent last night in one of his beds.

But what was Caprice Kincaid doing here? And why was she asking questions about Malcolm Lockhart?

"Gotta go, Janet." His steps were already taking him from the postal counter. He strode up the aisle and reached the checkout just as the exit doors swung shut behind his quarry.

Pausing impatiently, he watched through the plate glass doors till she got into her car. As soon as she drove out of the car park he made for his Range Rover.

And he followed her, at a distance, as she took the river road north—the route he took to go to the lodge.

She drove steadily, and in less than ten minutes he could see the Ryland's Resort sign. When he noticed her left turn signal blink, irritation coursed through him. Did the woman think he would let her stay at the lodge again tonight? No way! But even as he glowered at the Honda, it sailed past the entrance...

And turned, a few seconds later, onto the track that led through the forest to the old Lockhart place.

After dinner that evening, Will stood on the crest of the hill, staring with delight at the smoke puffing from Holly Cottage.

"Fang!" She kneeled down to hug him. "The first summer lady's here!" She snuggled her cheek against his velvety ear. "But we can't go visit her till Dad goes away, and that won't be for at least two more weeks—"

"Hey!"

Will almost jumped out of her skin when her father's voice came from behind her. Shooting upright, she whirled. "Dad! I thought you were watching the six o'clock news!"

He was staring at the puffs of gray smoke. "I have to go down there."

"But Lockhart land's off-limits!"

"It *is* off-limits...but this is just a one-shot deal. That lady who stayed over last night—"

"Mrs. Kincaid?"

He nodded. "I believe she may be staying at Holly Cottage, and I need to talk to her."

Willow's eyes widened. "*She's* one of the summer ladies?"

"Seems that way."

"Why do you need to talk to her?"

"I told her I didn't want her to pay for her room, but she left money anyway, and I want to return it because—"

"Because if she's one of the Lockhart summer ladies, she's going to need it. They're usually poor, aren't they?" Even as she spoke, Will's mind was racing. If her dad went down there and Mrs. Kincaid invited him in, he might see the drawings on the fridge. Oh, cripes, she was going to be in the biggest trouble she'd ever been in her life!

"Dad," she said in a rush, "if you give me the money, I'll run down and give it to Mrs. Kincaid."

"We'll both go...but we won't take Fang. I wouldn't want him to get confused—he knows it's a rule that he can't go beyond the fence, and it wouldn't be fair to allow it tonight and then change the rule back again tomorrow."

"Oh, Dad, you and your rules!" But Will wasn't even thinking about his rules—or how confused Fang must be already, because she'd taken him beyond the fence more times than she could count! All she could think about was what might happen if her dad got inside Holly Cottage.

Caprice was in the kitchen tidying up after dinner when someone hammered loudly on the back door.

Startled, she paused, a dish towel in her hand. Who could it be? Setting down the towel, she peeked out the window above the sink and saw Gabe Ryland and his daughter standing on the step. What on earth did they want?

She unlocked the door and opened it. Will was nervously curling a finger around a strand of her yellow hair; her father's rugged face was set in a dark frown.

"Hi," Caprice greeted them warily. "How can I help you?"

"You can help me—" Gabe thrust a narrow roll of bills at her "—by taking this back. I told you I don't want your money—"

"And," Will added, "you prob'ly can use it. The Lockhart summer ladies gen'r'lly find it hard to make ends meet."

Ah. They thought she was here courtesy of Break Away.

"How did you track me down?" she asked.

Gabe's eyes fixed on her steadily. "I heard in the village that you'd been asking about Malcolm Lockhart and I thought that was odd, because I got the impression last night that you were a stranger just passing through. But later I saw you drive in here, and I figured you'd been asking about Lockhart because you wanted to know more about the man who let the Break Away group use his cottage."

Caprice hesitated. If she told him who she was, how could she explain having asked the postmistress about Malcolm Lockhart? Besides, wouldn't it make her quest easier if she let the locals believe she *was* from Break Away? People in small communities often shut out strangers who asked questions. The postmistress had been proof of that.

"This is a very good place," Will said, "to have a holiday. You can have nice walks in the woods, and along the riverside path. We can't get to the river from our place, which is a *real* sore point with my dad because—"

"Will." Her father's interruption was brusque. "Mrs.

Kincaid doesn't want to hear about my problems.'' He thrust out the roll of notes again. "Here. Take it."

Caprice realized that if she did she would be lying by omission and confirming Gabe's belief that she was from Break Away. But sometimes, she told herself, the end justified the means.

Squashing her feelings of guilt, she took the money. "Thanks. But please let me repay you in my own way for your hospitality. Would you both come for dinner tomorrow night?"

Will's eyes flew wide open, and to her surprise Caprice saw a flash of panic in them. Panic that faded when her father said, "I appreciate the offer but this is a busy time for me, getting ready for the next batch of guests."

"You do have to eat," Caprice said. "And I won't mind if you leave right after. I'm a very good cook," she added. "Will did indicate that you have a...limited repertoire."

A reluctant smile flickered briefly around his lips then disappeared. "Yeah. But I *am* going to be busy."

"Well." Caprice adopted a teasing tone. "I plan on making lemon meringue pie for dessert, so if you happen to change your mind, come on down. If not, maybe Will could come by herself."

Before Will could respond, Gabe set his hand firmly on the child's shoulder. "I need Will to help me."

Although the child slumped with disappointment, she didn't argue. And meekly followed her father as he left.

Caprice went inside. She felt as disappointed as Will, but for a different reason. If Gabe Ryland had accepted her invitation, she could have slipped her father's name into the conversation, just to see where it might lead.

Now she was at a dead end again.

* * *

"Why couldn't we go to Mrs. Kincaid's for dinner, Dad?"

Gabe lifted Will off the top of the stile. Taking her hand, he walked with her up the grassy slope. "She was just being polite. Besides, I don't want to get involved."

"Because she's a Lockhart summer lady?"

"Because she's on Lockhart property."

"How come you don't like the Lockharts?"

He looked at her, and seeing the serious expression in her eyes, decided it was maybe time to tell her a bit of the family history. "It goes back a long way, honey. Malcolm Lockhart owns Holly Cottage now, but years and years ago, your great-grandpa Judd Ryland not only owned this place up here, he owned the Lockhart property, too."

"He *did?*"

"Yup. But he lost Holly Cottage and the riverside acreage in a poker game to Drew Lockhart, who was Malcolm Lockhart's father. Judd and Drew had been best friends till that happened—Drew worked for your great-grandpa and had the use of Holly Cottage—but after the game, your great-grandpa accused Lockhart of cheating. They had a big fight, and Lockhart took out a gun and shot your great-grandpa—"

"Did he kill him?" Will's eyes were wide.

"Uh-uh, he just shot him in the leg. Anyways, the case ended up in the courts and the judge sent Drew Lockhart to jail for six months for the shooting...but he ruled that Lockhart had won the land fair and square in the poker game. After he got out of prison, Drew Lockhart moved into Holly Cottage. But your great-grandpa Judd still swore he'd been cheated out of the land, and the Rylands and the Lockharts have been sworn enemies ever since."

They had reached the crest of the hill, and Will halted. Swiveling around, she gazed at the chimney tops of Holly Cottage and was silent for several thoughtful moments. Then she looked at him, her eyes puzzled.

"I can understand," she said slowly, "why Great-grandpa Judd would be so mad at Drew Lockhart, but how can *you* be mad at somebody you didn't even know...and for something that happened such a long long time ago?"

"There's a bit more to it," Gabe said. And that was an understatement! "But I've told you enough to be going on with. When you're older, I'll tell you the rest."

"Is it still about Great-grandpa Judd and Drew?"

He shook his head. "No, honey, it's about my father and my mother and Malcolm Lockhart."

Caprice spent the evening poking around in Holly Cottage, hoping to find some personal items belonging to her father, items that might help shed some light on his secret.

The ground floor consisted of the gloomy kitchen, a small bedroom—the one she had chosen to use—and a bright sitting room that overlooked the river. Upstairs there were two larger bedrooms and a bathroom.

Despondently, she ended up at one of the upstairs bedroom windows, staring out over the river, whose waters rippled peacefully against the sturdy wooden dock. She had found nothing in the cottage to help in her quest. The only items of any interest had been in the kitchen, and they had nothing to do with Malcolm Lockhart—a collection of drawings plastered to the fridge with magnets.

They were the work of a child. Each garishly colored sketch was of a different young woman, her name printed in felt pen at the top of the page. Emily. Sally. Adrienne. Juanita. Rosie. Ling. Janice.

And each drawing had three things in common. The subject was cuddling a dog that looked remarkably like Fang. The setting was the kitchen at Holly Cottage with its blue Formica table, wood stove and cushioned rocking chair. And the artist's signature was printed at the foot of the page. Willow Ryland.

Willow. What a pretty name, Caprice reflected. Why on earth had her father shortened it to Will?

But what Caprice found even more puzzling was the fact that the little girl had undoubtedly spent time in Holly Cottage. Yet only that morning Will had told her she wasn't allowed on Lockhart property. Caprice frowned as she recalled the look of panic in the child's eyes when Caprice had issued the dinner invitation to father and daughter. Had Will been afraid her dad would see the pictures?

Will must have been coming to Holly Cottage regularly in the summer months without her father's knowledge when Break Away clients were here. Caprice found the idea intriguing. And if she ever got the opportunity, she decided, she would ask Will to explain why she had so blatantly disobeyed one of her father's strictest rules.

Next morning, Caprice woke at six-thirty, and after showering and dressing in jeans and a pretty striped turtleneck sweater, she wandered to the river, her hands wrapped around her coffee mug.

She was standing at the end of the dock, watching the brisk breeze ripple the water's surface, when she heard a shout. Turning, she saw Will racing toward her.

She stopped breathlessly when she reached Caprice. ''Mrs. Kincaid,'' she blurted, ''can you do me a favor?''

"Will, good morning! I thought you weren't allowed to come down here—"

"I'm not supposed to! But I had to come down to get my pictures back! They *are* still on the fridge, aren't they?" she asked, her eyes wide with anxiety.

"Oh, yes, they're still there."

"Then can I have them please?"

"Of course."

Caprice led the child into the cottage, and as she gathered the drawings, she said to Will, "Did you often come down here to visit the ladies?"

"As often as I could...but only when Dad was away. I knew I'd get into big trouble if he found out...but for me it was worth it. And for Fang, too. He makes sad people feel better—dogs do that, you know."

What a courageous little girl, risking punishment and her father's displeasure to help people in need. Caprice felt guilty as she handed over the pictures. Will believed her to be one of those needy women; how she hated deceiving the child.

"Thanks." Will stuffed the papers inside her sweatshirt. "And thanks for inviting us for dinner. I didn't want to come in case my dad saw the pictures. But now they're down, I wish I could eat dinner here! Lemon pie's my favorite dessert. It's my dad's favorite, too, only he can't make it. He tried once, but it was like eating cardboard and yellow glue!"

Chuckling, they went outside and the child made to leave.

Caprice touched her arm to detain her. "Will, do you know why your father doesn't want you on Lockhart property?"

"There's a family feud, Mrs. Kincaid. My dad told me yesterday. It's from a long long time ago, like the

Hatfields and the McCoys that we've read about in school.''

''Ah,'' Caprice murmured. ''I see.''

Will took off but stopped halfway down the path and turned. ''My dad's mad at the Lockharts for something else.''

''What's that?''

''He says I'm not old enough to know about it. But he said there was some kind of a fight between his mom and dad and Malcolm Lockhart.'' Her watch beeped. ''Cripes, gotta go. Thanks again for the drawings.''

After the child had scooted away Caprice lingered at the door. So there had been a conflict of some kind between her father and Gabe's parents. It must have been serious for Gabe's hostility to have endured for so many years.

Could this conflict have been the reason her father had drawn a veil over his early background? What had happened between him and the Rylands that was so terrible Malcolm Lockhart had kept it a secret from his only child? And where did the mysterious Angela fit in?

Caprice leaned against the doorjamb, the early sun warming her face and the river breeze lifting her hair as she ran over the facts in her possession and considered what her course of action should be.

She seemed to have two options. She could spend days, even weeks, getting to know the locals and sounding them out. And maybe learn nothing at the end of that time. Or she could go to Gabe Ryland and try to ease the facts out of him without revealing that she was a Lockhart. She'd have to be very careful not to give herself away. His hostility to her family obviously ran deep; and Lord only knew what his reaction would be if he ever found out she was Malcolm Lockhart's daughter.

"That was pretty good, Dad. Really."

Gabe grinned as he poured water into the scorched pan. "On a scale of one to ten," he said, "I'd put it at a four."

"But last time you made grilled cheese sandwiches, they were only a two," she said stoutly. "You're *improving*."

"There's room! So…what would you like for dessert?" He opened the fridge and looked in, shook his head, opened the freezer section. "I guess we could have ice cream."

"Sure." Will's tone was too bright.

"I know. We've had ice cream every night this—"

The back doorbell rang, and he raised his eyebrows. "Who could that be?"

Will jumped from her chair. "I'll see." She ran across the kitchen and swung open the door. "Oh, hi, Mrs. Kincaid!" She gave a skip of delight and spun to him. "Dad, it's Mrs. Kincaid. Come here, quick…this you've *gotta* see!"

Gabe walked to the door and saw Caprice Kincaid hovering outside. She was carrying a pie in a Pyrex plate. The meringue looked mouthwateringly scrumptious.

She held out the plate. "You wouldn't come down for dinner," she said, "so I've brought dessert up to you."

"We can take it, Dad, can't we?" Will asked eagerly.

He hesitated. He really didn't want to get involved with this woman—but how could he refuse without being rude?

"It really wasn't necessary," he said. "But…thanks. We'll enjoy it, for sure."

As he accepted the pie, Will said, "But you haven't even cut a slice out for yourself, Mrs. Kincaid. She'll have to come in and eat with us, Dad. Right?"

Caprice shook her head. "Oh, no, really." She was wearing her hair loose, and the movement made it glide over her shoulders like a slice of sunshine. "I made it for you." She smiled at him—and as their eyes met and locked, something happened to him.

Something indefinable, but something that threw him completely off balance. A sizzling awareness…a sexual awareness. Sharp, electrical, thrilling. And as unexpected as it was unwelcome. Reeling from it, he somehow found his voice, somehow managed to keep it steady and casual.

"You must come in," he said. "I insist."

"Come on, Mrs. Kincaid." Will took her hand, gave it a demanding tug. "Let's cut this delicious pie!"

She tugged her lower lip with the tips of her pearly teeth. Then, after a brief hesitation, she gave a rueful smile.

"All right. Thanks, I'll stay."

She walked past him into the kitchen…leaving her perfume in her wake. Carnation and amber. Spicy and sophisticated. And sexy as hell. He blinked and stared after her, at her luxuriant blond hair, her curvy little figure, the catlike elegance of her walk.

Dammit, how come he hadn't realized before how attractive she was? He'd dismissed her as a pale, skinny blonde who wasn't worth a second look. Not that he was looking for a woman, anyway. Lord, no, that was the *last* thing he needed in his life. Once had been enough.

Or so he'd thought.

And now?

He walked into the kitchen like a robot, still shaking from the unexpected thunderbolt of attraction.

"Sit down, Dad!" Will handed a knife to Caprice. "This is going to be amazing!"

It was indeed amazing.

But not as amazing, Gabe thought, as the woman who had created it.

She was sitting across from him, her gray eyes alight with laughter at a joke Will was telling her. Will was laughing, too, and it occurred to him that it was three years since he and his daughter had sat here, at this kitchen table, with a woman who wasn't an employee.

And although the women who worked for him were all good people, they were also a bunch of tough cookies. He often worried about the influence they had on Will. And he also worried that she spent too much time with Mark. Heck, she even dressed like a boy! What she needed in her life was someone who could bring out her feminine side. Someone just like...Caprice Kincaid.

But he certainly couldn't see *this* woman fitting in at Ryland's Resort over the long term. Whatever the trauma that had made her one of Lockhart's summer ladies, she wasn't tough. When Will had asked her a few minutes ago why she hadn't stayed at Holly Cottage the night she'd arrived in the valley, she'd admitted, with a blush and an embarrassed smile, that a bird had scared her away. A bird! It had boggled his mind. She was the quintessential city girl, and city girls didn't last in Hidden Valley.

He'd learned that the hard way.

"Dad!" Will waved a hand in front of his face, and he saw she had already finished her slice of pie. "May

I be excused? I have to give Mark back his computer game tomorrow and I want to play it one last time. Okay?''

''Sure.'' He took in a deep breath, tried to get his thoughts in order. ''Yes, you do that, honey.''

She took off, leaving him alone with this dangerously attractive stranger who had stolen his breath away.

And as he stared at Caprice Kincaid, he wanted to get up and run for his life, because he knew, he just *knew,* that this woman, this highly unsuitable woman, had it within her power to go one step further and steal his very heart.

CHAPTER FOUR

"I'LL make the coffee." Caprice rose to her feet.

"I'll make it, I know where everything—"

"Let me." She waved him back into his seat. "I'm used to finding my way around a kitchen."

And he soon found out that she was.

After getting the coffee dripping, she moved easily to the table, cleared the dishes away, wiped the table, set a mug in front of him and one at her own place.

"Tell me," she said, leaning back against the island and curving her fingers around the lip of the island top. "How did your Outward Bound operation get started?"

It was both a joy and a torture to look at her. The joy came from the sweetness of her face, the torture from the tempting curve of her breasts. He fixed his gaze firmly on her face. Joy he could cope with; torture was something else.

"My grandfather, and then my father, ran this place as an inn. And after I finished high school, I worked with my dad. But innkeeping was never my cup of tea— I enjoy the outdoor life, so after Dad died, I changed direction. And what I'm doing now—every day's an adventure, and I have to admit that more than anything else, I love a challenge! I like to confront problems head-on and work them out. Or die trying! It's something I've tried to instill in Will. A person can do most anything, if they want to badly enough."

The coffee had finished dripping, so Caprice brought over the carafe. As she filled his mug, her arm brushed his shoulder and her scent again filled his head. He swallowed. Hard. The kitchen seemed suddenly to have shrunk.

And if she came that close to him again, he wasn't sure he could stop from grabbing her. Keeping his distance from her was one challenge he had to wonder if he was up to!

She'd just put the carafe back in place when Fang trotted into the kitchen and uttered a short, sharp bark.

Gabe snatched at the chance to get out into the open. Maybe the breeze would blow her perfume—and his lecherous thoughts—away.

He stood. "Fang wants a run. Take your coffee. Let's go out and have a walk before the evening cools off."

But once outside, he found himself still intensely aware of her...and thinking how delicately built and fragile she was. He wondered what personal trauma had made her an eligible candidate for a Break Away holiday.

He wanted to ask but was reluctant to pry in case his questions distressed her. So he confined himself to saying, as they ambled down the grassy slope in front of the lodge, "How long are you going to be staying at Holly Cottage?"

She paused and looked down over the treetops toward the log house. "I'm not sure yet."

"They've left it up to you?"

"They? Oh... Break Away." She took a few sips from her mug before saying, "Yes, it's been...left open. I lost my father recently...that's why I'm here. He'd been ill for a couple of years, and that put me under a lot of stress. A holiday seemed to be in order—time alone, time to regroup."

"You were close?"

"Very."

"What about your husband?" Dammit, he hadn't meant to pry. The question had shot out before he could stop it.

"I'm divorced."

"You're young to be—"

"We married when I was just nineteen. It didn't work out. The marriage lasted less than two years."

"Children?"

She shook her head. "I'm totally on my own now."

They stood in silence for a while, drinking their coffee, watching Fang frolic. Caprice broke the silence.

"This is such a pretty spot," she said, and added, out of the blue, "I wonder why Malcolm Lockhart would ever have wanted to leave it?"

Gabe gulped down the last of his coffee, which suddenly tasted as bitter as his thoughts. "Fresh fields, I guess," he said vaguely. He was not about to tell her the real reason. It was something he never spoke about—even after all these years, it was too painful.

"When did he leave?"

"Twenty-nine years ago."

"Did he ever come back?"

"Not that I know of."

"Odd," she mused, "that he never sold the cottage."

And went on, before he could come up with some way to change the subject, "What did Will mean when she said it was a sore spot that you didn't have access to the river?"

He tamped down the flare of anger her question had fired. Her curiosity was natural and innocent; he mustn't vent his frustration and resentment on her.

"When I take my clients white-water rafting," he said, "I have to drive them fifty miles up the valley to

Jackson's Landing—I rent a shed up there by the river to store the rafts—and it's a damned nuisance, to put it mildly, but I have no option.''

"Can't you get access somewhere nearer?"

"No."

"What about down there by Holly Cottage? It would be perfect, wouldn't it? Did you ever approach the owner, ask him if he'd sell the property or lease it or even give you a right-of-way?"

Ask Malcolm Lockhart for anything? He barely managed to suppress a contemptuous laugh. He'd sooner die than be beholden to that—

"Dad!" Will's voice came from behind. "Phone call!"

He clamped his jaw. Thank heaven for a timely interruption. Turning, he called to Will, who was standing on the crest of the slope, "Be right there!"

She waved and took off.

He turned to Caprice and said in a tone that gave away nothing of his churning thoughts, "Sorry, I have to go."

"I should be getting back to Holly Cottage now anyway." She held out her empty mug. "But thanks for letting me join you and Will for dessert. It was fun."

And she was beautiful. The breeze had brought healthy color to her cheeks, and stars sparkled in her smoky gray eyes. As he took the mug, her perfume drifted to him, carnation and amber, and he knew that whenever he smelled that provocative scent in future, he would think of her.

But she would not be in his life.

"It was also the best pie I ever tasted!" he said with cheerful lightness. And added casually as he took his leave and started up the slope, "If you ever need a reference as a cook...I'm your guy!"

*   *   *

His words brought a glow to Caprice's heart.

But they also unsettled her. And they were still with her that night as she lay in bed, trying to sleep.

Why was it, she wondered, that a simple compliment had made her feel so restless? It was by no means the first time someone had praised her cooking. After all, she'd taken a Cordon Bleu course in Paris after high school and had honed her skills over the past several years while acting as hostess at her father's frequent dinner parties.

No, compliments on her cooking were nothing new to her. Why then had Gabe Ryland's thrown her so off balance?

It wasn't till she was almost asleep that the answer came to her. It wasn't his praise of her cooking that was making her feel so restless, it was what he'd added. "If you ever need a reference as a cook...I'm your guy."

I'm your guy.

He wasn't her guy...but he must surely be someone's guy. He was charismatic and incredibly good-looking, and it would be naive to think he didn't have a woman in his life.

So why was she wasting her time thinking about him? *Get a grip!* she warned herself fiercely as she punched her pillow and turned it over. Even if he wasn't already spoken for, no way would Gabe Ryland want anything to do with her if he knew she was from the Lockhart family he so despised.

Rain started during the night, and when Gabe drove Mark and Will to school next morning, the weather was still wet and dull.

But Will's mood was bright as sunshine.

"Don't forget to drop by Mrs. Kincaid's on your way

home, Dad, and return her pie plate." She gave her father a happy peck on the cheek before jumping from the
Range Rover, close on Mark's heels. "She may need
it."

"Right." He let the engine idle. "Have a great day!"

"You, too!" Screwing her nose up against the rain,
she tugged the peak of her scarlet baseball cap over her
brow then raced off with Mark into the school grounds.

He waited and watched her, as he always did, not just
to satisfy himself that she got safely into the building,
but for the sheer kick he got out of looking at her.

His whole life revolved around his daughter—and the
responsibility that went with bringing a child up alone.
He frowned as he noticed, with a feeling of shock, that
she was outgrowing the yellow raincoat he'd bought her
last fall. Last time she'd worn it he could have sworn it
reached to the tips of her rubber boots; now it barely
covered her behind!

She was growing. And she was growing up.

He felt a jolt of panic. Before he knew it, she would
no longer be a little girl. How would he cope with her
as she moved into adolescence? If she'd been a boy, he'd
have known how to talk to her, what to tell her. But she
wasn't a boy, and one day she would emerge from that
tough cocoon she'd built around herself when her
mother deserted her, and come to him for information
and guidance, because she'd have no one else to turn to.
No female.

And what could he say to her, when that time came?

She disappeared into the building, and determinedly
tucking his worry into the back of his mind, he set the
vehicle in motion. The problem wasn't immediate; he
had time to work out some answers.

And now...he was going to return Caprice Kincaid's

pie plate. If he didn't, she'd eventually haul herself to the lodge to collect it. And he didn't want that, because he didn't want to get involved with her. And by dropping the plate off, he had control. When he spoke to her, he'd be pleasant without being too friendly, and he'd be out of there before she had time to blink.

And that would put an end to that.

He was on the brink of falling for her, but he'd be crazy to give in to his attraction. Caprice Kincaid had three glaring strikes against her. She was beautiful, she was soft and she was from the city. He had already experienced the grief her kind of woman could bring him.

And he had no desire to travel that route again.

"Help!" Caprice dragged her fingers through her hair and looked beseechingly heavenward. "Someone please help—"

As if in answer to her call, someone rapped abruptly on the back door.

She froze. Then, uncoiling herself from her crouching position at the kitchen's wood stove—the kitchen's stubborn, uncooperative, old-fashioned wood stove—she crept to the window and peeked out.

Oh, rats! Gabe Ryland was the last person she wanted to catch her in her robe and slippers. Heavens, she hadn't even had her shower yet!

But the only thing to do was carry it off with flair.

Hastily finger combing her hair from her face, she opened the door to a morning that had been left green and fresh after a heavy rain that was tapering away.

Her visitor was wearing a navy crew neck sweater and jeans, and he was carrying her pie plate.

"Good morning." She adopted her welcoming-hostess smile, the one she'd used to greet her father's business colleagues when they and their spouses came to dine at Lockhart House. "I see you've brought back my plate."

His gaze flicked from her face to her hair, and he blinked. "I've heard of déjà vu—" amusement threaded his voice "—but this is ridiculous!" He leaned in, set her plate on the countertop and took her hands in his. "Tell me—" he uncurled her fingers and looked at the palms "—were you a chimney sweep in a previous life?"

Her hands were black. With soot from the stove. And she must have transferred some to her hair, to her face.

"You're having a problem—" his eyes glinted "—with your wood stove?"

Not as big a problem as she was having with his sexy grin. And the closeness of his big, rugged body. And his earthy male scent. And the intimate touch of his callused fingertips on her palms.

Swallowing, she slid her hands free and wrapped her arms around her waist, shivering as the breeze from outside cut through the flimsy pink silk of her robe. "I'll manage."

"I'm sure you will," he drawled, "but by the time you do, it may be too late. You may never get yourself thawed out again." He shouldered the door shut. "I'll have a look at it."

She hesitated for a moment and then forced out a reluctant thanks. She stood back to let him enter.

He glanced around. "Gloomy in here." The only window was above the sink, and it was half blocked from outside by an overgrown holly tree. "It'd be brighter with those branches pruned back."

He moved to the stove, crouched and looked in through the side-loading door. And immediately saw why she wasn't getting the stove going. She'd used logs that were too big, logs that had little chance of catching till the fire had a good base. Removing them and setting them aside, he tugged a newspaper from an adjacent wicker basket.

As he coiled sheets into nests, he said, "With those holly branches gone, you'd not only get more light, you'd also catch the morning sun and get a bit of extra warmth."

"I've already made arrangements to get it done. I phoned the caretaker yesterday—"

"Maura Adams."

"You know her?"

Gabe stuffed the nests into the stove and arranged a neat wigwam of kindling over them. "Everybody in Hidden Valley knows everybody else in the area. Got a match?"

She slipped the pack from her pocket and tossed it to him. "Anyway," she went on as he touched a flame to paper, "I phoned Mrs. Adams, and she said the man who was supposed to look after the gardens had moved away but her husband, Sean, was looking for part-time yard work. So I hired him. He starts tomorrow morning, first thing."

Gabe blinked. Wasn't she taking rather a lot on herself? Slamming the stove door shut, he stood up and said, in a questioning and faintly critical tone, "You called the Break Away group first, to get their approval?"

"I don't think that's any of your business!"

Touchy, touchy! He lifted one shoulder in an if-you-say-so shrug, then crossed to the sink. He washed his hands, and when he turned, he saw she'd moved to the stove and was standing there with her back to him.

Her shoulders were trembling.

Dammit. He could have kicked himself. Here was a woman who'd just lost her father and was dealing with Lord only knew what other traumas or problems, and he'd chided her for assuming responsibility at a time when even a small step like that had probably loomed enormous to her.

He closed the space between them, took her by the shoulders and turned her to face him. "Look, I know this isn't an easy time for you, and it must be really hard to make decisions. I should have congratulated you for taking the initiative, instead of which I—"

"It's all right." Her gray eyes glistened, but they had a stubborn glint that defied him to argue the point. "Trust me, I wasn't doing anything out of line."

Under the thin silk of her pink robe, her skin was marble cold. "You're freezing!" Frowning, he ran his hands up and down her upper arms. "You should have a hot shower, get yourself warmed up."

"I will, now that you've got the stove going." Her smile was wan and somewhat self-deprecatory. "I was determined not to let it beat me and I've been struggling with it for the past half hour. I really appreciate your help—knight in shining armor coming to the rescue!"

Rubbing her arms, warming her skin, had released her body scent, a sleepy bedtime scent that mingled with the faintest drift of her carnation and amber perfume. He found the blend tantalizingly erotic. And all at once he was hit by an intense urge to drag her against him, nuzzle his face into the curve of her neck, press his mouth to her creamy skin and inhale her intoxicating essence.

He managed to control himself but couldn't resist placing the back of his fingers gently against her cheek.

"Glad to be of service," he murmured. "Every beautiful woman should have a white knight at her beck and call."

Her eyelids flickered. And under his hand he felt a rush of blood heat her cheek. "Every woman should learn to look after herself." Her eyes were steady. "So that she doesn't have to wait around for a white knight." There was no mistaking the cynicism in her tone as she added, "White knights aren't always what they're cracked up to be."

"Obviously," he murmured, "you've learned that the hard way. Your ex?"

He took her silence for a yes.

"Was the breakup a...mutual decision?"

"No."

"So...one of you walked."

"I did."

Why did that not surprise him? He'd already warned himself not to get involved with her. And yet when she'd opened the door, he'd found himself teetering at the top of the slippery slope to love. Not to mention lust. And what red-blooded male wouldn't have, at sight of blond tousled hair, misty gray eyes and that curvy little figure wrapped in shimmery pink silk? He'd almost groaned aloud. Only the soot had saved him. It had allowed him to make a joke, to cover his bedazzlement. He had fooled her, but he hadn't fooled himself. And he'd walked as eagerly into the cottage as a child drawn into a candy store.

But this piece of candy was not for him.

And fortunately she had—without realizing it—reminded him of that fact by confessing that she was the one who had walked out on her marriage.

Oh, he was well aware that he had a blind spot where broken promises were concerned. But he was only human, and humans are what their past has made them. Marriage, in his book, was forever. But the wedding vow—that most sacred vow of all—obviously meant nothing to Caprice Kincaid.

Just as it had meant nothing to his ex-wife.

The fire was crackling promisingly, and there was nothing to keep him here.

He stepped back, jamming his hands into his pockets.

"I'll be going." He kept his tone casual. "You need to have that shower. And by the time you're dressed, the chill should be off the kitchen."

He walked away, but turned at the doorway. She was standing exactly where he'd left her. And she looked so fragile and so forlorn and so very alone he ached to stride back, gather her in his arms, tell her he'd look after her, for now and forever more....

"In case we don't meet again," he said briskly, "I hope you have a great holiday, and that when you go home, you'll be strong and well, and ready to make a fresh start."

After he'd gone, Caprice expelled a shaky breath.

How shocked he'd be if he knew the effect he had on her. As he'd stood at the door, looking across at her as he said his goodbyes, she'd desperately wanted him to come back, to gather her up in his arms, hold her close.

It had been sheer torture when he'd caressed her cheek with the back of his hand. It had sent all sorts of sensations tingling through her, making her melty and weak. It was so long since she'd been kissed, and she'd wanted—desperately wanted—Gabe Ryland to kiss her.

And for a moment, she thought he might.

But his attitude had changed, had hardened, when she'd told him she was the one who had walked out on her marriage. He obviously hadn't approved of that. For whatever reason. At any rate, he had made it clear he didn't want to see her again. His brush-off had been polite but unmistakable.

And she couldn't even put matters right and get back on their previous friendly footing, at least, other than by telling him the reason she had walked out on Liam.

And she couldn't do that without revealing who she was. And if she blew her cover she might never get the answers she needed. The answers she needed before she could put her father, and his past, to rest.

Next day dawned warm and sunny, and the gardener, Sean Adams, arrived early. Caprice told him what she wanted him to do in the gardens, and he immediately set to work. He appeared to be surly and uncommunicative, but she planned to quiz him—discreetly—about her father and the Rylands, and was hopeful she might get some answers.

Mid-morning, she brought him a mug of coffee and a fresh-baked blueberry muffin—a bribe, she acknowledged to herself guiltily—and when he sat down on a tree stump by the back door to enjoy them, she lingered on the step.

"Your wife," she said casually, "has been caretaker here for some time?"

"Aye." Munching on his muffin, he gazed morosely at the forest.

"She got the job from Malcolm Lockhart himself?"

"Aye."

"She knew him, before he left the valley?"

"Aye."

She was getting nowhere fast. Time for a bolder move. "Mr. Ryland has been quite kind to me since I arrived. Will, his daughter, mentioned that there had been some kind of a feud between the two families.''

''Aye.'' He sipped noisily from his coffee mug.

Mentally, Caprice rolled her eyes. But threading her tone with faint amusement she went on, ''Kind of quaint, don't you think? Like something out of a storybook. You don't happen to know what it was about, this feud?''

''Aye. I know the whole story.'' He fixed her with a pair of rheumy blue eyes—rheumy eyes that glinted with cunning. Caprice held her breath. Was she at last going to learn something? She waited, her pulse skipping faster.

''But I'm not about to discuss it with you or with any other Nosey Parker stranger. It was a family affair, missy, and it was nobody's business but their own!''

Getting to his feet, he poured the rest of his coffee onto the lawn and insolently tossed the last half of his muffin to the birds. He picked up his secateurs and shuffled across the grass to an overgrown forsythia bush by the gate. And with a contemptuous snort, he went back to work.

Caprice felt like kicking the old sourpuss in the seat of his patched denim pants, but she managed to suppress the urge. She would get nothing out of Sean Adams; that much was obvious. He was even more reticent than the village postmistress.

She heaved a frustrated sigh as she went into the cottage. If she wanted to obtain information about her father and the Rylands, she would have to look elsewhere.

And look elsewhere she did.

During the following week she frequented the village and many of the other hamlets in the area, poking around touristy stores and initiating conversations at the drop of a hat. But though the locals were all friendly enough, as soon as she tried to talk about Malcolm Lockhart, she came up against a solid steel wall.

By the time Sunday rolled around, she found herself thinking she'd set herself an impossible task, and in an effort to raise her spirits, she decided to take a break from her detective work and go to the village church.

The minister was sincere, his sermon uplifting, the music restorative. By the time the service was over, Caprice felt refreshed and more than prepared to resume her investigations.

But as she was going out the church doors, the minister pulled her aside, a look of concern on his lined face.

''Folks around here,'' he murmured gently, ''all know you've been snooping, Mrs. Kincaid, and I have to tell you, they don't like it. They don't like outsiders coming in and raking up the past. The feud between the Rylands and the Lockharts—well, the locals all like Gabe Ryland and they all feel very protective of him. Now you may have good reasons for asking your questions, but there's only one person that folks feel has the right to give you answers.''

''And that person is?'' But Caprice already knew what he was going to say.

''That's Gabe Ryland himself.''

Early next morning, Caprice packed her bags and tucked them into the Honda's trunk.

She was going to leave the valley today, but before she did, she was going to make one last attempt to get the answers she wanted. And if it meant bearding Gabe Ryland in his den and confessing who she was, then so be it. She had come to Hidden Valley with a mission and she couldn't go home without approaching the one

man who might be able to answer her questions. Of
course, he might not talk to her, but at least she would
have done her best—

"Mrs. Kincaid!"

She turned from the car and saw Will racing toward
her. Alarm shot through her at sight of the child's pan-
icked expression.

"Will, what on earth's the matter?"

"It's my dad!" Will cried wildly. "He's asleep, and
I can't get him to wake up!"

CHAPTER FIVE

CAPRICE bundled the child into the Honda and threw herself into the driver's seat. "We'll take the car," she said. "It'll be faster."

"Dad's breathing real rough!" Will's voice shook.

"Was he all right last night?" Caprice set the vehicle in motion, and the Honda shot down the track.

"He was coughing a lot the last couple of days, and I think he had pains in his chest, 'cause he kept bending over. And then he went to bed early last night. He never even wanted to eat dinner."

"We'll phone the doctor." Caprice tried to sound calm and reassuring. "Do you have the number?"

"It's by the kitchen phone. But I came down for you," Will added in an anxious rush, "because I know Dad would be mad at me if I called Dr. Grant—he hates seeing doctors even more'n he hates being sick!"

"He may well hate seeing doctors," Caprice returned grimly, "but in this case, he's not going to have a choice."

On reaching the lodge, they wasted no time in getting inside and hurrying to the family's private quarters. They passed the kitchen, and next to it Caprice caught a glimpse, through an open doorway, of a comfortably furnished sitting room. Across from it was a closed door.

Will made for it. "He's in here," she whispered. And opened the door quietly.

The bedroom was large and airy, with a bay window. The venetian blinds were half open, and the morning sun

slanted across the gray carpet and onto the king-size bed,
forming yellow slats on the white sheet—Gabe's only
covering. It was rumpled and pushed down to his waist;
his duvet was on the floor. He was sprawled facedown.
Sweat formed a heavy sheen on his back and plastered
his hair to his nape.

Frowning, Caprice crossed quickly to the bed and felt
a jolt of alarm when she saw that Gabe was shaking.
She touched her fingertips to his back. His skin was ice-
cold.

Hiding her concern, she said to Will, "Sweetie, get
me a towel." As the child ran into the en suite bathroom,
Caprice shook Gabe's arm. "Gabe." She spoke urgently. "Gabe, wake up!"

The only response was a low protesting moan.

Will raced in with a white terry towel, and Caprice
swiftly mopped Gabe's back and nape before hauling the
duvet from the floor and wrapping it over him and tucking him in.

"There," she said, "that's all we can do for him right
now. Let's go to the kitchen and phone for the doc."

Dr. Grant turned out to be a gangly young man with
orange hair, a long neck and a brusque manner.

Caprice and Will hovered outside the bedroom while
he examined his patient. When he emerged, he was tucking a cell phone into the pocket of his gray tweed jacket.

"I've called for an ambulance," he said, "to take Mr.
Ryland to St. Paul's Hospital in Cedarville. I want to
run some tests. I suspect he may have a touch of pneumonia."

"Then will he have to stay in hospital, Dr. Grant?"
Will's face looked pinched.

"Can't say for sure. But if he's able to come home, would there be someone here to look after him?"

"Mrs. Kincaid *might* be able to." Will looked at Caprice with a pleading expression.

The doctor raised his eyebrows in question.

Caprice paused, but only for a beat. "Yes. If it's necessary, of course I can stay on."

She felt Will's small hand creep into hers, and this sign of the child's trust brought a lump to her throat. As she closed her fingers tightly around the little hand, she vowed not to leave the valley till Gabe was well.

Dr. Grant phoned in the early afternoon.

He reported that his patient did indeed have a touch of pneumonia. He added that he had phoned a prescription in to the village pharmacy, which Caprice should pick up.

"The ambulance will be leaving here shortly," he said. "Make sure Mr. Ryland gets to bed right away. Call me any time—day or night—if he takes a turn for the worse. And I'd like to see him in my office on Monday."

Caprice and Will popped down to pick up Gabe's medication, and when they came back, Caprice brought in her overnight bag and her case.

"I should sleep in your family quarters if you have a spare room," she said to Will. "So I can keep a good eye on your father."

"Oh, we do have one extra bedroom," Will said, and led her to a room next to her father's bedroom.

She crossed to the window and opened the venetian blinds, revealing a pretty room with a powder blue quilt and pale oak modern furniture. Then she crossed to the en suite bathroom, and with a frown of concentration gazed around it.

"Everything's ready," she said as she turned. "Fresh towels and soap and shampoo and conditioner." She moved to the double bed and bounced up and down on the mattress. "I've never slept in here, but it seems comfy enough." Her expression was anxious. "Is it okay for you?"

"It's perfect!" Caprice dropped her case and overnight bag on the cream carpet. "Now come help me unpack. I'd like to get all settled in before your dad gets back."

The ambulance arrived when Caprice was arranging her toiletries in the powder blue and cream bathroom. Will, who'd been watching at the bedroom window, saw it first.

"He's here! Come on, Mrs. Kincaid, let's go meet him!"

They hurried to the lodge's main entrance, and when Caprice opened the door, she saw two medics carrying Gabe, on a stretcher, up the front steps.

He looked to be asleep.

She led them to his bedroom, with Will bringing up the rear. The patient murmured a protest and opened his eyes blearily as the attendants transferred him to his bed, and Caprice stole the opportunity to administer one of his pills, after which he immediately drifted off again. She escorted the medics out, and when she returned to the bedroom, Will was standing by the bed, looking at her sleeping father. His breathing was still heavy, and the pallor of his face was accentuated by the charcoal dark stubble on his jaw.

He looked very vulnerable, Caprice reflected as she

joined Will by the bed, vulnerable and weak...but still irresistibly attractive. And he looked so alone on that big, wide mattress. How easy it would be—and how tempting a notion—to slip in beside him....

"Mrs. Kincaid?"

Will's voice jolted her from her foolish and totally inappropriate fantasy.

"Yes, sweetie?" she said, talking to Will over her shoulder as she moved to the window and closed the slats of the venetian blind, casting the room into deep shadow.

"What should we do now?"

"We let your dad sleep. Sleep, they say, is the best healer. But in case he awakens soon, we'll leave the door ajar and keep a good eye on him. I'm going to the kitchen to make our dinner. Would you like to help?"

"I'd like to, but I have to do some piano practice. For a school concert," she added, as they slipped from the room. "It's going to be in the village hall, on Friday night. I have to do a solo. And it's really hard."

"If you need any help, let me know." Caprice smiled. "I've been playing piano for as long as I can remember."

"Really?" Will's eyes shone. "After you make dinner, could you come and show me how to do this specially difficult bit? I'll be in the guests' lounge."

Gabe drifted out of a deep sleep to the sound of Mozart.

The music was so faint, on the edges of the dream he'd been having—a dream or a memory?—of being hustled around in a dazzlingly bright room while he tried to emerge from a stupor and listen to what Dr. Grant was telling him. He remembered he'd been in a hospital, and vaguely remembered being carried into an ambulance for the trip home.

He was in his own bed; he knew it because he could feel Fang's familiar weight against his legs. He moved his feet and felt the weight lift off. Then he felt paws padding up the bed and felt Fang's rough tongue on his hand before the dog jumped to the carpet and lolloped away.

One thing he *did* remember was Dr. Grant telling him he had pneumonia—just a mild case, but it had knocked the stuffing out of him. Heck, he couldn't argue with that!

He heard Fang bark somewhere in the lodge—the sharp bark the dog used when he wanted someone to pay attention.

The sound of Mozart halted abruptly.

And even as he lay there, wanting to get up but not having the strength, he sensed someone coming into the room.

"Dad."

It was Will. He could just make out her form as she approached the bed.

She leaned her hands on the edge of the mattress. "Are you awake?" she whispered. "Fang came to fetch us."

Us? Who the devil was—

"Hi." The softness of a woman's voice enfolded him like a fuzzy blanket. "How are you feeling now? We were just about to waken you. It's time for your next pill."

"Mrs. Kincaid?" He could see her hovering behind Will. "What the hell," he asked groggily, "are you doing here?"

"Dad!" Will's tone was chiding. "You mustn't say—"

"Sorry." He sighed. "It just slipped out. What the heck is Mrs. Kincaid doing here? In my bedroom?"

"Dad, you would still be in the hospital if Mrs. Kincaid hadn't agreed to stay on and look after you."

"Agreed with whom?"

"It was my idea. But Dr. Grant said you wouldn't get to come home if there wasn't someone here to look after you."

"And who called Dr. Grant, young lady?" Gabe faked a scowl.

"Mrs. Kincaid."

"And how did Mrs. Kincaid find out I needed a doctor?"

Will screwed up her nose. "Don't be mad at me, Dad. I know I'm not supposed to go on Lockhart land, but when I couldn't get you to wake up this morning, I ran down to Holly Cottage for Mrs. Kincaid and we drove up here real fast and that's when she phoned Dr. Grant. *Are* you mad at me?"

He had barely the energy to lift his arm, but he managed, and he ruffled her hair affectionately. "I'm proud of you for showing initiative, honey. You did well."

She beamed.

Mrs. Kincaid moved to the window and flicked the blind half open, letting golden rays of sunshine flow in. As she walked back, the brightness backlit her, and for a few moments all he could see was the outline of her curvy figure. Desire sizzled through him with an unexpectedness and an intensity that made him gasp. To cover up, he coughed, but once started, he couldn't stop.

Next thing he knew, Caprice was holding a glass of

water to his lips. He gulped some water, and some more, and finally the coughing fit passed.

By the time it did, his lustful impulse had passed, too. And he was left feeling wiped...and astounded that he could have been beset by such carnal urges when he was so sick.

Sinking back on his pillow, he closed his eyes.

"Dr. Grant prescribed some medication. Will and I picked it up. It's almost time for you to have a pill," Caprice said. "Can I tempt you into having a bowl of soup first?"

Less than a minute ago, she could have tempted him into something much more appetizing than a bowl of soup. He shook his head. "Thanks, but I'm not hungry."

"I'll get the pills, Dad, they're in the kitchen."

As Will spoke, the phone rang in the kitchen. "I'll get that," she said, and she took off.

Opening his eyes, Gabe said, "Mrs. Kincaid—"

"Caprice."

"Caprice. How come the phone in here isn't ringing, too?"

"I unplugged it before you came home so you could sleep and not be interrupted."

"Thoughtful of you...and kind of you to act as nursemaid. I appreciate it. And I'm indebted to you."

"I owed you one. You took me in last week when I needed a place to spend the night. We're even now."

"I'm not sure I agree with that. But anyway, I'll be up and about by tomorrow, and you can get back to being on your own."

"I'm not in any hurry," she said, "to be on my own."

"But isn't that why you came to the valley?"

She paused before saying, "Yes, but...I enjoy spending time with Will. She's a delightful child."

''How about me?'' His voice seemed to come from far away, and he knew he was drifting off to sleep again. ''Do you find me delightful, too?''

''Delightful? I think interesting would be a more appropriate description. Maybe even…complex.''

''Uh-uh, I'm a simple guy, Caprice. Whatcha see—'' his words were slurring ''—is whatcha get. Now you…you're different. You're a woman, and women are all mysterious, they all have secrets. What secrets are *you* hiding?''

But he wasn't about to get an answer to his teasing question, because at that moment, Will raced into the room.

''Sorry I took so long.'' She handed Caprice the pill container. ''I was trying to get this open but—''

''It's childproof, Will.'' Caprice twisted the lid off. ''Who was on the phone?''

''Mark's mother. She wanted to know if I could come down and play with Mark.''

''Is she still on the line?''

''Yup.''

''Gabe?'' Caprice's voice echoed in his head. ''Is it okay?''

''Sure.''

Will said, ''Goody. His mom told me she'd pick me up after dinner. I'll go tell her it's okay.''

Caprice gave Gabe his pill, which he washed down with the rest of the water. As she reached down to take his empty glass, her hair swung forward and brushed his hand.

Clumsily, he ran his fingers into the glossy swath, twisted his wrist, and she was captured.

He heard her breath catch. ''What do you want?''

What he wanted was to have her slide into bed with

him. "What I'd like—" his voice was trailing away "—is for you to come back later so we can have a cozy little talk."

"About what?"

"About all your little secrets..."

"They wouldn't be secrets anymore if I were to share them with you! But I might share one or two of them," she added, "if you share one or two of yours. You could start by telling me what you have against the Lockharts."

"How d'you know I have anything against them?"

"I got that impression from Will. You've apparently forbidden her to step foot on Lockhart land."

"That's right," he said drowsily, "I have. And you're right, I don't like the Lockharts. Okay, Mrs. Kincaid, you've got yourself a deal. Come back later—" his fingers slid from her hair "—and I'll tell you the whole story of the Lockhart-Ryland family feud!"

After Will left with Mark and his mother, Caprice peeked around Gabe's door, but saw that he was asleep. As she crept away, she felt a stab of frustration. It had seemed she was on the verge of finding out something of her father's past. And perhaps something about Angela. Now, she was forced to contain her impatience.

Mark's mother dropped Will off at nine and stayed to chat. Her name was Merrily, and she told Caprice over a cup of tea that as well as helping her husband on the farm, she had just opened a hairdressing salon in the farmhouse basement.

"I'd love to get my hands on Will's hair," she confided to Caprice as Will and Mark gave Fang a run outside. "I could do wonders with it, but she's a stubborn little thing and refuses to let me near it."

"One day maybe." Caprice smiled. "When she's older."

"She tells me you're on holiday in the valley and just helping out here while her dad's ill."

"Mmm, I've been staying at Holly Cottage." Caprice's heartbeats quickened as she realized that here was a golden opportunity to ask a local some questions about her father. "The cottage is owned by a man called Malcolm Lockhart," she said. "Apparently he used to live in the area. Did you happen to know him?"

"We've only lived in the valley for a year. Bob and I moved to the farm after his uncle died. I don't know too many people yet, we've been so busy with the farm. But Bob hired an extra hand last month, so I was able to open my beauty salon—I'm a hairdresser by trade. I'm sure I'll soon get to know lots of people once I'm established. But till now we haven't mixed, and I can't say as I've ever heard the name Malcolm Lockhart."

Hiding her disappointment, Caprice listened as Merrily chatted about her new business till Will and Mark came indoors and Merrily rose to go.

After Mark and his mother left, Caprice put Will to bed. She stayed up till midnight, when she crept into Gabe's room to give him his next pill.

There was just enough light slanting in from the hall to let her see that he was asleep. She woke him to feed him his pill, and then watched him fall right back to sleep.

She went to bed then, exhausted after her long day, and was out like a light within minutes.

Gabe woke to the sound of someone padding across the bedroom carpet.

He squinted into the shadowy dark and saw Caprice by the bed.

"Hi." His voice was rusty with sleep. "What time is it?"

"It's morning. Six o'clock. Time for your pill."

"Thanks." He shoved himself up on his elbow.

"How are you feeling?" She handed him his pill.

"Like a new man. I'll be up and about before you know it." After swallowing the pill, he slumped onto the pillow. As he did, he was struck by a vague memory of their last conversation, a conversation in which he'd promised to tell her why he hated the Lockharts. He must have been really out of it. No way was he going to discuss that with her or anyone else!

She crossed to the window, and flicking the blind open a fraction, let the gray dawn filter in. "Now," she said as she turned again, "you really should have something to eat. What do you fancy?"

"What I fancy—" he couldn't keep the amusement from his tone "—is for you to come to bed."

He saw her blink with shock, but her quick recovery was admirable. "In your dreams, Mr. Ryland," she returned briskly. "And if you don't tell me what you want for breakfast, you'll have to take pot luck!"

"Speaking of dreams," he said, "you starred in mine last night. You were walking on a beach—somewhere hot and sunny—and heads were turning because you were wearing only the skimpiest of—"

"Enough. It's not good for you, in your weakened state, to be dwelling on your erotic fantasies!" She turned on her heel and stalked toward the door. "And I can tell you, I find *nothing* more boring than other people's dreams!"

"Heck, this dream wasn't boring! Not with you cavorting around the way you were, in a teensy black feather bikini and—''

She slammed the door on his words.

He laughed. And lacing his fingers behind his head, he looked at the ceiling and let his mind drift back.

It really had been one hell of a dream.

And who would ever have thought he would end up in bed with the woman of his dreams ministering to him! He'd been trying his damnedest to banish Caprice Kincaid from his mind ever since he'd bade her a firm goodbye last week.

Now Fate had tossed her back into his life.

And who was he to try to outwit Fate!

Caprice cooked Gabe two lightly boiled eggs, toasted a couple of slices of whole-wheat bread and added a glass of orange juice and a mug of steaming coffee to his tray.

She walked into his bedroom just as he was emerging—rather unsteadily—from the bathroom. He was wearing only a pair of briefs in black knit cotton, the formfitting style leaving very little to the imagination. And she'd always had an extremely fertile imagination....

When he saw her, he grinned. ''You've come back to hear the rest of my dream?''

''No, I have *not* come back to hear the rest of your dream.'' But she knew that he'd probably end up in her own dreams that night. She'd never seen such a fantastic body. Leanly muscled. Powerful. Virile.

And if she'd been a Victorian lady given to the vapors, she'd have collapsed right there and then, caring not a jot if she spilled coffee and juice all over the carpet.

''You look,'' he drawled, ''as if you're rooted to the

spot. I didn't realize I was such a startling sight. But I must say, your reaction to my half-naked body is doing wonders for my...ego!''

She blinked, and realized she was standing gawking at him with her mouth open.

She snapped it shut, set her body in motion and directed it to the night table. "You took me by surprise," she muttered. "I didn't expect to see you up."

He laughed outright, and as she realized what she'd said, her face turned scarlet. He was still chuckling as he got into bed, and she was struck by a sudden urge to empty his coffee mug over his head.

She avoided looking at his face as she set the tray on his lap, but she couldn't avoid the minty smell of his toothpaste and the clean smell of soap—mundane scents, yet their very ordinariness spelled out an intimacy between them that made her throat turn dry.

"Thanks," he said. And his breath fanned her cheek.

Her own breath caught, and she moved quickly away from him to the window, giving her heartbeats a few moments to steady, while she opened the blind fully.

The sun was gliding up over the mountaintops, painting gaudy crimson streaks over the milky blue sky, and she saw that it was going to be a glorious day. Through the open window she could smell the fresh, pine-scented air, and she could hear the distant cry of a rooster, followed by a dove's mournful whoo-oo from the nearby woods.

She swallowed to relieve the tightness of her throat before saying brightly, "The sounds of the countryside are so different from the sounds of the city."

"You miss the city."

He wasn't asking a question, but making a flat statement. And his tone had a cynical edge.

She turned. His jaw was more roughly stubbled than ever, but despite the scruffy effect, he looked much better than he had last night. And even more knee-bucklingly sexy and hazardous to her heart. "Did I say that?"

He shrugged. "Once a city gal, always a city gal."

"What do you have against city girls?"

"Oh, I have nothing against them, as long as they stay where they belong." With his knife, he knocked the top off an egg. "And where they belong is sure as hell not in Hidden Valley! Might as well plop a duck in the desert! How long have you lived in Seattle?"

Caprice hesitated. If she told him she didn't live in Seattle but Chicago, he'd surely think it strange that Break Away had brought her here from out of state. But she didn't want to lie. She had already practiced enough deception—

Fang's sharp bark from the hall saved the moment.

"Oh, excuse me." She hurried across the room to the door. "I'll have to let the dog out before he wakes Will."

She let Fang out, and when she came inside, she went to close Will's bedroom door. Last night, the child had set out her clothing for the morning, and Caprice noticed yesterday's outfit lying on the carpet by the dresser.

She tiptoed in to pick it up. But as she did, she saw a gold brooch glinting on the child's striped T-shirt.

She smiled. So Will wasn't the one-hundred-percent tomboy she purported to be. She did like jewelry and wasn't above wearing it on the sly!

But Caprice's smile faded, and her heart gave a frightening thump against her ribs, when she saw that the pretty gold brooch spelled out a name.

And the name that it spelled out was Angela.

CHAPTER SIX

WILL came into the kitchen at seven, yawning as she fastened the bib straps of her blue denim overalls. "Good morning, Mrs. Kincaid. Did you let Fang out?"

"Good morning, Will." Caprice turned from the sink, where she was scraping Gabe's empty eggshells into the garbage disposal. "Yes, I did."

The child slipped into her seat. "I looked in on Dad but he's sleeping. Is he feeling better?"

"Much. He ate a good breakfast."

Will poured cereal and milk into her bowl. "Do you think he'll be able to get up today?"

"If he's anything like most men, it'll be impossible to keep him in bed once he's strong enough to stand up without falling over! But he'll have to take it easy for a while."

Will dug her spoon into her cereal bowl. "What about my concert on Friday night? That's only three days away! What am I going to do if he's not well enough to take me?"

"If he's not well enough then I'll still be here, and I'll take you."

"Promise?"

"Promise."

"Will you come to the concert anyway, even if my dad's better?"

Caprice opened her mouth to say she'd no longer be in the valley if he was better, but before she could speak, Will went on in a brave but wistful voice.

"Sometimes it's truly hard, Mrs. Kincaid, not having a mom. If you came to the concert with my dad, then I could pretend…just for one night…that I'm in a real family."

Memories of her own school days crowded into Caprice's mind, memories of concerts and other special events when her father had sat alone, and her heart had ached for both him and for the mother she had loved and lost.

Surely she could do this one small thing for a child who gave so much to others at great risk to herself and with no reward other than the satisfaction of brightening up the weary lives of unhappy Break Away moms.

"Will, I'd love to come to your concert."

"Oh, goody!" Will reached for her juice glass. "I'm so—" She broke off with a gasp, and froze. Her eyes were fixed with glazed horror on the brooch, which Caprice had earlier set in the middle of the table. Tension twanged around the kitchen for several long moments, and then the child raised apprehensive eyes to Caprice. "Where…where did that come from?"

Astonished by the child's over-the-top reaction, Caprice asked, "Don't you know?"

Will gulped, and her cheeks grew scarlet. She shifted her gaze to her cereal bowl, and stammered, in an almost inaudible voice, "From my T-shirt."

Caprice sat next to her, and tipping a finger under the child's chin, tilted her face up. "What's wrong, Will? Why are you so upset?"

"Does Dad know? Did you tell him about the brooch?"

"No. But whose is it? And where did you get it?"

Will blinked back her tears. "You won't tell my dad?"

"Why don't you explain, first, why it has to be a secret."

Will's gaze was troubled as she searched Caprice's eyes, obviously trying to determine if she could be trusted. At last, she heaved out a sigh. "All right. I'll explain. But for now, I have to hide the brooch. Okay?"

"Go ahead."

Will retrieved the brooch and stuffed it into her pocket. "There's something you've gotta see, Mrs. Kincaid, and then you'll understand. But there isn't time just now. Mark's mom'll be here soon to pick me up for school so it'll have to wait till I get home. It *has* to stay a secret from my dad, though, because if he found out where I go and what I do, he'd probably never speak to me again!"

As the morning went by, Caprice could hardly contain her impatience. What a stroke of luck finding the brooch. It looked as if she was close to learning who the mysterious Angela was. And once she knew, there was nothing to keep her in the valley…other than her promise to Will.

She wouldn't, of course, desert Gabe, either, if he needed her, but that remained to be seen.

He slept all morning, but woke around noon, at which time she gave him his pill. As he handed back the empty water glass, she said, "I'll bring your lunch now—"

"Have you eaten yet?"

She shook her head.

"Then eat here with me."

"Oh, I'll have mine in the kitchen—"

"Then so will I." With a challenging glitter in his eyes, he made to sweep back the bedcovers. Hastily, she said, "All right." Not only did she believe he'd be better staying in bed, the last thing she wanted was another viewing of his half-naked body. "I'll eat with you."

She had prepared a salmon and celery quiche, along with a green salad, and after serving his, she brought her meal on a small tray, along with two mugs of coffee, and sat on a chair by his bed while they ate.

"So," Gabe said after a while, "how was Will this morning?"

"She was worried about getting to her concert on Friday. I told her I'd drive her if you weren't better."

"Oh, thanks, but I'll be okay by then."

Caprice hesitated before saying, "Will has invited me to come, too. I hope that's okay with you?"

"Sure. You'll enjoy it. Some of the older kids—the music they make is amazing. And of course I'm looking forward to hearing Will play. By the way," he added, "yesterday I woke to the sound of Mozart. That was you?"

"I'd been helping Will with her concert piece—she asked me to play something for her."

"You're one very talented lady. When did you start playing?"

"My mother was an accomplished pianist, and some of my earliest memories are of sitting at the piano with her while she taught me the notes. She died when I was five, but my father saw to it that I had lessons...even when money was tight. He always said it was important to get one's priorities right, and in his view, music was right up there."

"A sensible guy."

"He was. And a very kind and gentle one." Caprice's smile was nostalgic. "He was a New Age Man before the term was even invented!"

"Then you were a lucky girl."

"I know. But you're bringing Will up the same way. You're a wonderful dad…and she just adores you."

"It's a two-way street, Caprice. She's a great kid and the most important person in my life." He drank the last of his coffee and set the empty mug on his tray. "Tell me more about your father."

Caprice shifted uncomfortably on her chair. By talking about her father, she would be perpetuating her deception. But it was a catch-22. If Gabe knew who she was, he'd kick her out of his home so fast she wouldn't have time to blink. And which was more important, coming clean with Gabe or finding out about Angela? It was no contest.

Even as she made the decision, Gabe asked,

"What did he do for a living?"

Caprice finished her coffee and moved her tray from her lap to the night table. "He started off by buying an old house," she said. "A handyman's special. After renovating it, he sold it and made a tidy profit. Then he bought a couple more, and eventually invested in a small apartment building. He soon had a good business going."

"You miss him?"

"Terribly. I also miss the structure he gave my life. I feel as if I'm floating—adrift, as it were, on the ocean, yet hoping that there's land out there somewhere and I'll finally get to it."

"I had the same sort of feeling when my own father died. Then land appeared—at least I thought it was solid land but it turned out to be a mirage…."

Relieved that he'd turned the conversation to his life, she relaxed and waited for him to go on.

"My wife," he explained. "I met her a couple of months after my father passed away." His laugh was bitter. "She wasn't dry land, after all. More like sinking sands."

"How long had you been married before she died?"

"Died? The woman, as far as I know, is still very much alive! What made you think she—"

"Will." Caprice looked at him, bewildered. "She told me her mother had died three years ago."

"Good Lord." He raked a hand through his hair, and it stood up in funny spiky tufts on the crown. "Why the heck would she have told you that?"

"I have no idea."

"She knows full well that her mother took off. She actually saw her leave! The kid was inconsolable. For weeks!"

"You mean—"

"Deirdre and I are divorced. She's remarried and living the high life in L.A. with some hotshot movie producer. She's never so much as sent Will a postcard since she walked out, and before she *did* leave—" his expression was hard "—the only interest she had in her daughter was dressing her up like a doll."

They sat in silence for a few moments, and then Caprice said quietly, "Where did your wife meet this man she's married to now?"

"He came to Ryland's for the skiing. Filthy rich, and made sure everybody around him knew it. Deirdre had dollar signs in her eyes from the moment they met...and when he left after ten days, she left with him." He gave a dry laugh. "My ex-wife was, first and last, a city girl. My mistake was in believing her when she claimed— before I married her—that she'd learn to love country life. But she never made the effort. I guess it's true, a leopard can't change its spots. Once a city gal, always a city gal."

He'd used that same cynical expression before when talking about city girls. Caprice wanted to resent it, but she could only feel sorry for him. He had been hurt, and the wounds were still unhealed. She noticed that he looked very pale and drawn. Talking—and perhaps his bitter emotions—had exhausted him.

She got to her feet, removed his tray and set it with hers on the night table. "That's enough chatting for now—you're supposed to be taking it easy. Lift your head, I'll fix your pillows."

He elbowed himself up while she plumped his pillows, then he slid down on his back. She felt him watching her as she smoothed his covers, and she tensed as he caught her by the left wrist.

"I'm curious to know," he murmured, "why—when you're no longer married to the guy—you still wear his ring."

"I wear it," she returned pertly, "because it gives men the impression that I'm unavailable. Especially men on the prowl—" pointedly she extricated her wrist from his grasp "—who can't keep their hands to themselves!"

His laugh was spontaneous. "Touché." But his face quickly sobered. "So you're going to spend the rest of your life without…male companionship?"

"I didn't say that."

"But you're not ready for another relationship."

"I didn't say that, either."

"Ah. So you're just going to keep floating till you see dry land. Well, take my advice, my dear Mrs. Kincaid, and don't take a flying leap at it without checking it carefully first, just in case what you think is terra firma turns out to be nothing more than sinking sands."

*   *   *

Will was going directly to her piano lesson in the village after school and, as arranged, Caprice picked her up there in the Honda when the lesson was over.

The child's face looked a little pinched, and instead of greeting Caprice in her usual cheery manner, she gave her a brief hi before slumping in her seat.

"Had a tough day?" Caprice asked, glancing at her as they drove off.

"It was okay. How's Dad?"

"He was asleep when I left. But he's feeling a lot better and he's planning to get up when he wakes again."

She'd expected Will to be happy with this news. Instead, she retreated into silence. Something had happened to upset her, Caprice reflected. And she resolved to get to the root of it later—but she'd wait till after dinner, when they had their time alone and Will showed her whatever it was that would explain where she got the brooch.

It was only with difficulty that Caprice managed to tamp down her escalating excitement and anticipation.

When they got home, they found Gabe in the sitting room, watching TV. He was wearing black cords and a black turtleneck sweater, and though he had shaved he still looked ruggedly dangerous. Caprice's heartbeats revved into overdrive as she looked at him. Every time she saw him, she became more attracted to him. Will was lucky—she could do what Caprice ached to do...fall into Gabe's arms!

But contrary to Caprice's expectations, the child didn't run over and hug her father. She hung back in the doorway.

"Hi, Dad. Are you better?"

Caprice thought he still looked drawn, but he said heartily, "I feel great. So...where's my hug?"

After the briefest hesitation, Will crossed the room and leaning over, hugged him.

He hugged her back, and then held her away from him, smiling. "So...how did piano practice go?"

Caprice saw a shadow darken Will's face. The child shifted her gaze to Fang, who was snoozing by the hearth.

"Okay. Mrs. Norton's going to phone this evening about the concert. I *told* her you'd been in the hospital and you were sick and couldn't speak to her but she asked who was looking after me and I said Mrs. Kincaid so she said she'd talk to *her.*"

Before Gabe could comment, she said, "I have to do my homework now," and took off without waiting for a response.

Gabe cocked an eyebrow in Caprice's direction.

"Your guess is as good as mine," Caprice murmured. "I think she's just had a bad day."

But she silently renewed her resolve to have a talk with Will after dinner to try to find out what the problem was.

Gabe joined them for the evening meal, but as soon as Will had finished eating, she pushed her chair back and asked to be excused.

"I have to practice my piano piece for the concert. And then I have to finish my homework."

She scooted off, and as soon as she was out of earshot, Gabe said to Caprice, "What the heck's going on?"

"I don't know." Caprice started clearing the table. "She was fine this morning when she left with Mark's mom for school, but when I picked her up at Mrs.

Norton's, she was awfully quiet. Maybe she's worried about the concert. After all, it must be quite an ordeal for a child to be up on a platform alone, performing for an audience.''

''Yeah, but she's not a shy kid. She's never been backward in coming forward. It's just...something's not quite right.''

''I'm planning to have a talk with her as soon as I've cleared up here.'' Caprice tucked the dishes into the dishwasher and clicked the door shut. When she turned, she saw that Gabe was rising from the table.

''Thanks, I'd appreciate that. And thanks, by the way, for a terrific dinner. You're spoiling me.''

She smiled and said lightly, ''You're worth spoiling.''

His eyes darkened, and she sensed a sudden electrical snap in the atmosphere. He moved toward her with deliberate intent in his step. ''You enjoy spoiling me?''

She felt a rush of alarm—alarm and a breathless excitement that stole the air from her lungs.

''Cat got your tongue?'' he teased, his eyelids half-closed. He stopped close to her and settled his hands intimately on her hips. ''Maybe I could help you find it.''

She gasped, but he smothered it with a kiss. A kiss that tasted of coffee and heaven. Of Gabe himself. Intoxicating and irresistible. Even if she still had her voice, even if she'd been able to cry, ''Stop!'', she knew she wouldn't have meant it. His kiss was fire and tenderness, burning her and at the same time melting her. She wanted it to go on forever...and it might have, she thought, dazed, if a sudden ring of the doorbell hadn't interrupted it.

His arms tightened around her briefly, and then cursing under his breath, he drew back from her with obvious reluctance while she slid her arms from around his neck.

Breathing unevenly, he muttered, "Who the devil's that!"

Caprice avoided looking at him. Running tidying fingers through her hair, she made for the door.

"I don't know," she said. "But I'd better find out."

The caller was Will's music teacher.

After they had introduced themselves, Mrs. Norton said, "I thought that what I have to say would be better explained face-to-face, rather than over the phone."

Caprice's heartbeats were still racing from her passionate encounter with Gabe, but she forced it from her mind as she led the teacher to the sitting room. After offering refreshments, which the visitor refused, Caprice closed the door and sat down across from the sofa where Mrs. Norton had seated herself.

The other woman seemed ill at ease, so Caprice decided to take the bull by the horns. "Will seemed upset after her lesson today. Was there a problem?"

"There is...but not a major one," the teacher added quickly. "It's about...clothes. You see, Mrs. Kincaid, the concert on Friday is going to be a formal one. But Will told me this afternoon that she intends to wear jeans and a T-shirt, and she was adamant in her refusal to wear anything else. It would deeply distress me to exclude her from the event, but rules are rules. The girls are not allowed to wear jeans at the annual concert, and they never have been. To allow it now, for one child, would be to make an exception and set a very bad precedent."

Caprice breathed a soft sigh of relief. So that was all. "The other children...what will they be wearing?"

"The boys are to wear dark pants and a white shirt,

and the girls must wear either a dress or a skirt and blouse. Er, Mrs. Kincaid…'' The teacher hesitated.

''Yes?''

''There isn't a…problem, is there? Financially, I mean? If that's the case, then I would happily, out of my own pocket—''

''On, no, Mrs. Norton, that's not at all the case. I'm sure Will's father is well able to afford to buy a suitable outfit for her. But…isn't this rather short notice?''

''Each student was given a letter to take home weeks ago, and it spelled out the clothing requirements clearly.''

''I wonder if Will gave her father the letter?''

''Excuse me?''

''Sorry, I was talking to myself.'' Caprice stood. ''Mrs. Norton, leave this matter with me. I'm not sure why Will doesn't want to wear a dress, but I'll do my best to find out and set everything straight.''

After the teacher left, Caprice went to the lounge in the public part of the lodge. She found Will sitting at a coffee table, engrossed in her homework.

As Caprice entered, the child looked up.

''Sweetie.'' Caprice moved over to sit on the sofa beside her. ''Mrs. Norton has just been here—''

''I won't wear a dress.''

The determined glint in Will's eyes told Caprice she hadn't set herself an easy task. ''Why, Will? Is it such a terrible thing to wear a dress just for one night?''

Will snapped her schoolbook shut. ''Where's my dad?''

''He was in the kitchen before Mrs. Norton came. I'm not sure where he is now.''

''I need to show you something…what we talked

about this morning…but I can't, not while he's around. When is he going back to bed?''

''Why don't you wait here, and I'll go and find out?''

Hiding her puzzlement, Caprice went in search of Gabe. She wasn't looking forward to facing him again after their kiss, but there was no way around it. She found him in his bedroom. He was standing by the window, looking out. Nervously clearing her throat, she said, ''Gabe?''

He turned around, and she was startled to see how very pale he was. Pale and tired.

''You've stayed up too long,'' she said.

''Yeah, I guess. So, what did Mrs. N. want? I heard her voice,'' he explained, ''and hid in here.''

Caprice told him about her conversation, and finished by saying, ''I'm going to have a heart-to-heart with Will now, make her see that sometimes we just have to fit in with everybody else when there are rules to follow.''

''Well, I think we know how Will feels about rules! Good luck. The kid's a tomboy and seems determined to remain one.''

''I'll give it my best shot. In the meantime, I'd like you to get back into bed.''

''Your slightest wish is my command,'' he drawled. He added in a teasing tone that miraculously broke the tension she'd been feeling between them, ''But first I'm going to strip down to my underpants. Want to stay and watch?''

She laughed.

He laughed, too.

And she could still hear the echo of his chuckles as she made her way to the lounge.

*   *   *

"Just wait till you see what's in here!" Having led Mrs.
Kincaid to the attic, Will opened the old trunk and held
her breath as she waited for Mrs. Kincaid's response.
"Isn't this something?"

"My goodness, it certainly is! What a treasure trove!"

That was exactly the response Will had expected and
wanted. "That's not all!" Triumphantly, she lifted out
a pile of clothes and set it on the table. "Underneath,
there's shoes and scarves and hats...and jewelry." From
her pocket, she took the Angela brooch and laid it atop
a string of pink pearls. "I play dress up here all the
time!"

Mrs. Kincaid sank down on the rocking chair. "I
don't understand. I thought you didn't like pretty
clothes."

"Mrs. Kincaid, I just *love* pretty clothes!" With care,
Will returned the pile from the table to the trunk. "But
I can't ever wear any. Not in front of my dad!"

"Now you've *really* got me confused."

Will set a foot on the edge of the rocking chair and
used it to hoist herself onto the table. She sat cross-
legged at Mrs. Kincaid's eye level.

"It's a long story," she said. "And it goes right back
to when I was just four years old. I was actually seven
days past my fourth birthday when it all started. I told
you a lie when I said my mom was dead. I just say that
'cause I don't want people to know that she didn't love
me enough to take me with her."

She saw that Mrs. Kincaid wanted to speak but she
pressed on. "My mom took off one day with a man who
wasn't my dad. And my dad drank way too much that
night. I was in bed but I couldn't sleep because I was
crying so much, so I went to look for him and I heard

him in the sitting room but when I opened the door he was crying, too. He was sitting in an armchair, all slumped over. I could see an empty whiskey bottle on the table. And he was talking to himself, real loud and angry, about beautiful ladies, and how you couldn't trust them, and he'd never love anybody again, 'specially never anyone that was pretty. And that,'' she said, with a knowing nod, "was when I figured that if I wanted my dad to keep loving me, I had to make myself plain. And it's been real easy for me, Mrs. Kincaid, what with my raggedy yellow hair and funny eyes and turned-up nose. And of course,'' she added with scorn in her voice, "I never, *ever* wear pretty clothes. That would be about as dumb a thing as I could possibly do. So you can see now why I won't wear a dress to the concert. I know my dad loves me just the way I am, and I don't ever want that to change—''

She stopped short and frowned as she saw that Mrs. Kincaid was blinking real fast. "What's the matter?'' she asked curiously. "What did I say to make you cry?''

CHAPTER SEVEN

CAPRICE swallowed over the huge lump in her throat. She took the child's hands in hers and held them tight. "Will, thank you for telling me that story...and it's a really sad story in places, that's what brought tears to my eyes. But you're wrong, sweetie, about one thing. Your dad will *always* love you, no matter how you look or what you wear."

"But he said he wouldn't ever like pretty ladies."

Caprice hesitated, then said softly, "Will, do you think I'm pretty?"

"You are *truly* pretty. You have the prettiest hair and the prettiest eyes and the prettiest clothes and—"

"I want to tell you a secret. Just a little while ago, when you were doing your piano practice, your dad let me know that he liked me a lot. He even kissed me!"

"He *did?*"

"He truly did."

"Wow!" Will mulled this over. "So," she said at last, "do you think he'd still like me if I put on a pretty dress for the concert?"

"Trust me, your dad loves you because you're you, and he'd still love you no matter what you wore. Clothes are just like...well, the wrapping on a present. It's not really important. It's what's inside that counts. And that's what your dad loves about you."

Will's expression was doubtful. "You're sure?"

"I'm sure. Tell you what—how about I meet you right after school tomorrow and we drive to Cedarville and have a look at the dresses. Maybe we can find something you like, and then Mrs. Norton will be happy because you'll get to be in the concert.''

''Well…'' Will chewed her lip, and then she said slowly, ''We could *look* at the dresses…and if we find one that's not *way* too beautiful, Dad might not even notice.''

''It's a deal.'' Caprice gave Will a hug, and the child slid off the table.

''We'd better be going downstairs,'' she said. ''Just in case Dad wakes up and wonders where we are.''

''Will…it must have been someone in your family who owned these things in the trunk.'' Caprice took in a deep breath before asking the question she'd been bursting to ask from the moment she'd seen where the brooch came from. ''Do you know who she was?''

''Sure!''

''You do?'' Caprice hardly dared believe her ears. ''So…tell me!''

Will delved to the bottom of the trunk and pulled out a framed photograph. She handed it to Caprice. ''This,'' she said, ''is my grandad and my grandma on their wedding day. It says so on the back.''

Caprice's gaze flicked from the groom—who strongly resembled Gabe—to the bride. And when she looked at the radiant brunette in the white lace gown, her heart leaped, and she knew she'd come to the end of her search.

The woman in the picture was Angela.

Gabe stood at the open door and watched, unseen, as Caprice moved around the sitting room, tidying magazines, plumping cushions, stooping to pick up a computer game Will had left on the floor by the TV. She'd put the child to bed an hour ago, and ever since, she'd been avoiding him.

But why?

Was she embarrassed because of their kiss? She'd seemed to enjoy it at the time. But perhaps he'd moved too fast—or perhaps she figured the kiss had meant nothing to him, that it had been forgotten as soon as it was over.

Well, she was wrong about that. It certainly wasn't forgotten; in fact, he doubted he'd ever forget it. He could still hear the whisper of her surrender; could still taste the silken promise of her response. He'd wanted her more than he'd ever wanted anything in his life, and he still wanted her. It wasn't just physical attraction, either. It was more, so much more.

Did it scare him? You bet your boots it did! But he wasn't about to ignore it...or let her ignore it, either.

He walked purposefully into the room. ''Hi, there.''

She spun around, and he saw her eyes quickly take on a veiled expression. ''Oh, hi.''

He walked over and grasped her shoulders. ''This,'' he said, ''is where we left off.'' And he kissed her again—

Or rather, he tried to. Before he could make contact she'd wrenched away from him and taken a step back. She looked flustered, breathless, pink-cheeked...and defensive.

More than anything, defensive.

''Gabe, I'm not a...a toy, that you can pick up and play with whenever you feel like it!''

''Toys are for kids. I'm no kid, Caprice. I thought—'' his smile became teasing ''—you'd have noticed that by now.''

The color in her cheeks deepened. "You know what I mean!"

"No," he said. "I don't."

"You can't just go around grabbing people and—"

"You're not people. You're a woman. An extremely lovely and desirable woman…and one who, I believe, enjoyed our last kiss as much as I did. When two people feel this way, why fight it?"

"We don't even know one another!"

"You can live with someone for ten years and not know them or you can be with someone for ten minutes and feel—"

"Lust, Gabe. That's what this is about. Proximity lust. Nothing more."

"I don't think you believe that's true. But even if it were, we're both adults, so what's wrong with following up on the way we feel?"

"You mean…we should be like animals and just…mate?"

He chuckled. "Put that way, it doesn't sound very appealing, but—"

"What other way is there to look at it?"

"Okay. Let's take this more slowly. You want to get to know each other first? Fine. If you want us to be friends before we—"

"I'd like us to be friends, period."

He shot up his eyebrows. "You're not interested in taking it further? Is it something about me that you don't like, or—"

"I don't know anything about you, Gabe. Or at least, what I do know isn't enough to base even a friendship on, far less a more serious relationship."

"What more do you need to know? You know all about my life today. You want to know about my past, too? Okay, I'll go right back to my childhood. Hell, I'll even drag all the ancient skeletons from the closet and spill out the Ryland family's deepest secrets.''

Her eyes took on a startled look. But when she spoke, her tone was light. ''That's the second time you've promised to tell me all about the Ryland-Lockhart feud.''

He shrugged. ''It's not something I like to talk about, but if it'll get through this barrier you've set up—''

He broke off as Fang gave a sharp bark from the doorway. Looking around, he saw the dog standing there, his tail wagging, his eyes fixed on him steadily.

''He needs a run,'' Caprice said. ''I'll let him out.''

''We'll both go, get some fresh air.''

''But shouldn't you stay indoors? You don't want to risk catching a chill.''

''I'll be fine. It's not a bad night. And some stories,'' he added tersely, ''are better told in the dark.''

It *was* dark outside, and the air was swimming with the scents that only night can bring.

Caprice's thoughts swam, too, as she walked down the front steps with Gabe. If only he hadn't tried to kiss her again. She didn't want to fall in love with him, but he was making it very difficult not to.

Now that she knew the mysterious Angela was Gabe's mother, she was wary and apprehensive. And she wasn't about to let her relationship with Gabe go any further till she found out what the connection was between her father and the beautiful brunette.

What was Gabe going to tell her?

She didn't even know if his mother was still alive.

''Give me your hand.'' His voice came to her in the dusky night. ''I don't want to lose you.''

Her breath caught as her fingers were enfolded in his strong grasp. She'd felt nervous and apprehensive a moment ago; now she suddenly felt...safe.

The feeling was soul-deep. And she sensed, with a surety that was just as deep, that this was a man who would never let her down.

Gabe Ryland was a man she could trust.

And she prayed that what he was going to tell her was not something that would shatter the happiness Fate seemed to be dangling before her. She had lied when she told Gabe she wanted only to be friends. She had lied to protect herself from whatever she might find out now.

As they walked across the lawn in front of the lodge, she heard Fang blundering in the forest, heard a distant stereo beat from a car skimming by on the highway. And then she heard only Gabe's voice.

"It goes back," he began, "to when my father was a student at Cedarville High. He and Malcolm Lockhart had been best friends since kindergarten. The summer they turned sixteen, people called Kingston moved to Cedarville from L.A., and their daughter, Angela, enrolled at the school. That fall, the three ended up in the same grade...and before very long they became inseparable."

"What kind of person was she?" Caprice asked quietly.

"Every guy in school was crazy about her. She was clever and she was beautiful...and she was as popular with the girls as she was with the boys. At least, that's what I gleaned from my dad."

"So...he fell in love with her?"

"Like the proverbial ton of bricks."

"And...did Malcolm Lockhart fall in love with her, too?"

"According to my dad, he did."

Gabe sounded bitter. Caprice looked at him, but all she could see in the dark was the shape of his head and the breadth of his shoulders and the steely glint of his eyes

"And who—" she tried to keep her tone casual "—did Angela choose to love?"

"She married my father."

"So she was your mother."

"Right. But love?" He gave a cynical laugh. "The woman didn't know the *meaning* of the word."

They reached the edge of the forest and stopped walking. Caprice inhaled the piney smell of the trees...and the heady male scent of the man holding her hand. But for once it was easy to ignore it. She sensed that in the next few seconds, she was going to get all the answers to the questions that had been worrying at her.

She felt her stomach muscles clench. "So," she said, "tell me about those skeletons in the family cupboard."

"When I was seven—" he ran his hand up her arm and rested it at her nape "—my beautiful mother had an affair with Malcolm Lockhart—"

Shock pounded through Caprice. This was the last thing she'd expected. She barely managed to suppress a gasp.

"—and late one night he came and picked her up in his car and the two of them took off together. They hadn't gone more than sixty miles when another vehicle crossed the centerline and ran headlong into them. My mother was killed instantly."

"Oh, Gabe..." Caprice choked on the words. Choked on her compassion for him. Even as she shrank in horror from the knowledge of what her father had done. ''How awful...''

''Lockhart escaped with whiplash and a few bruises.'' His voice was laden with contempt. ''He never came back to the valley again. I believe that if he had, my father would have killed him. So there you have it, Caprice. That's my past and that's what drives and motivates me to hate the very name Lockhart. My dad never got over losing the only woman he'd ever loved. And I have never forgiven—nor will I ever forgive—the man who destroyed our family.''

Caprice's thoughts careened in turmoil as she struggled to recover from her shock. She could scarcely believe that her father had stolen another man's wife. It was so totally out of character. The Malcolm Lockhart she knew had been a man of unwavering morality.

When she'd found out he'd deceived her about his place of birth, it had bewildered her and unsettled her— but it had never occurred to her that the reason for his deception would have reflected so very badly on him. It pained her beyond words to know that he hadn't been the man she'd thought him to be.

She shuddered, and Gabe was immediately solicitous.

''Let's go in,'' he said. ''You're getting cold.''

She wasn't, but she didn't argue. Didn't dare argue, in case her voice gave away her distress.

Once inside, she wasn't really surprised when he didn't pick up on the conversation they'd been having before Fang interrupted them. Talking about the past had changed his mood, and she realized he'd withdrawn mentally.

Gathering herself together, she offered to make him a cup of tea, but he declined. Saying he was tired, he said good-night and took off in the direction of his bedroom.

Caprice went into the kitchen and made herself a mug of hot chocolate. Sipping it, she paced the room unhappily.

What she'd learned from Gabe had set her emotions awhirl, and she knew that dragging out the old story of his mother's betrayal had stirred up Gabe's emotions, too. But talking about such devastating events could sometimes be beneficial, and she hoped that having done so might in the end help ease some of Gabe's bitterness. She now knew, though, that there could never be anything between them. Not even friendship. *Especially* not friendship. Once he knew she was a Lockhart, all he'd feel for her would be a blinding rage that she'd used him.

The knowledge made her want to weep.

And it made her want to flee.

But she'd promised Will she'd stay for the concert, and she wasn't about to let the child down. In the meantime, she'd try to keep out of Gabe's way as best she could till the morning after the concert, at which point she would say her goodbyes to both him and his child.

But before she left she would dredge up her courage and tell him who she really was—not a Break Away client, as she'd led him to believe, but the daughter of his longtime enemy, the man who had stolen his mother—Malcolm Lockhart.

"I'm going to the village to pick up my mail." Gabe's voice came from the laundry room doorway. "Fancy a jaunt?"

Caprice turned from the dryer with a mound of warm Downy-scented clothes in her arms, and at sight of Gabe felt her heart ache with longing, just as it did every time she saw him. That morning he'd turned up for breakfast in his robe, and when she'd seen him her knees had wobbled. Now showered and shaved, dressed in a crisp white shirt and hip-hugging blue jeans, he was to die for.

"Thanks." She managed a casual smile. "But I have some ironing to do. Besides, it's almost noon. You go. I'll have lunch ready when you get back."

He crossed and took the bundle of laundry from her arms. "Play hooky with me." He tossed the clothes onto the ironing board. "It's glorious out—not a day to be wasted. After we get my mail, I'll take you out for lunch. To an old-world restaurant on the river—a converted mill. The food's unbelievable."

"No, I—"

"I won't take no for an answer." His green eyes twinkled, but his jaw was determinedly set. "I've already booked us a table."

Caprice caved in. Weakly caved in. The temptation was too great. Besides, she argued to herself, what was the harm? Surely she could keep him at bay in a crowded restaurant. "All right, just let me fold these clothes—"

"I'll fold them." He pushed her out of the room. "Get yourself ready, woman. We leave in five minutes."

The Mill Wheel Restaurant was halfway between Ryland's Resort and Cedarville. The car park was almost full, but Gabe found a spot near the entrance.

"We'll have a drink before we eat," he announced as they entered the foyer. "There's a cocktail lounge in here." He ushered her through open French doors, then across a pleasantly furnished room to a round table by the windows. "Let me take your jacket."

"Thanks." She noticed with a feeling of despair that as soon as he came within three feet of her she felt the spark of his chemistry. And when he touched her—his hand brushing her nape as he slid her jacket off—she was surprised the contact didn't make her flesh sizzle. Even after he'd seated her, she felt as breathless as if he'd whacked her in the stomach.

He, on the other hand, looked cool as a steel blade. Sitting across from her, he tossed his mail on the table. "I'll have a look at that, if you don't mind, after we've ordered our drinks. What'll you have?"

"Sherry, please. Dry."

He ordered a lager for himself, but after the waiter departed, he seemed in no hurry to get to his mail. Instead, he fixed his gaze on her—more specifically, on her charcoal gray knit top, with its short sleeves and roll collar. "You look great," he murmured, "in that color. It makes your eyes dark and sexy. And mysterious," he added with an intimate smile. "Full of secrets. Why do I always get the feeling that you're hiding something from me?"

Her heart lurched, but she gave an amused chuckle. "What could I possibly be hiding?"

"You tell me!" He picked up a letter and tapped it idly on the tabletop. "You've been in the valley for a couple of weeks, and I still know next to nothing about you. I know you're a city girl, I know your visit is sponsored by Break Away, I know you're divorced, and you've recently lost your father. That's it!"

"You also know I can cook." She clasped her hands on the table to stop her nervous fidgeting. "And you know I can—"

"Kiss." He grinned as she blushed. "And I know you're good with kids and you're good with invalids. But these are things anyone can see. What I want is to get to know the person underneath." His face became serious again. Reaching across the table, he cupped a warm hand over hers. "Ever since we kissed, things have changed. You've been shutting me out. Please don't. You and I, we could have—"

"Sherry for the lady." The waiter slid the crystal glass onto her coaster. "And your lager, sir." He paused, waiting for Gabe to draw aside so he could set down his drink.

Taking advantage of the moment, Caprice lifted her glass and sat back, out of Gabe's reach. While he paid for their drinks, she focused her attention resolutely on the view outside.

The windows overlooked the river, and the sun sent shimmering darts over the surface. On the opposite bank she could see white houses with lawns that ran right down to the water's edge, and a sliver of beach where an elderly couple strolled hand in hand.

"Cheers!"

She turned her attention to Gabe, who had raised his glass to her. She raised hers. "Good health."

The sherry was excellent, and she told him so. But when she sensed he was about to pick up their conversation where it had left off, she said quickly, "Why don't you have a look at your mail? It's been a few days since you've picked it up. There might be something important."

"Sure," he said. But she knew, by the glint in his eyes, that her respite was temporary.

He riffled through the envelopes, putting all aside but two. The first, he murmured as he scanned the contents, was from his top guide, Alex Tremaine. He slipped it into its envelope, along with an enclosed newspaper cutting. When he read the second letter, he frowned.

"Something wrong?" asked Caprice.

"It's from Lou Anders—my lawyer. I need to see him." He slid the letter into its envelope. "His office is in Cedarville. Do you mind if we take a run over there after lunch?"

"Will and I had planned an outing to Cedarville after school. Why don't you wait? We can all go together. You can meet Mr. Anders while we have a look around the stores."

He shrugged. "Sure. We can do that."

Before they could continue the discussion, the waiter came to tell them their table was ready, and they moved to the dining room to have their lunch.

Gabe was quiet while they ate. It was obvious to Caprice that his thoughts were elsewhere, and whatever the lawyer's letter contained, it was very much on his mind.

"Does Dad know that we're shopping for a dress?"

Caprice swung Will's hand in hers as they walked into the department store. "No, he didn't ask what we needed in town...so I didn't tell him!"

"Why does he need to see his lawyer?"

"He didn't say."

Will trailed her hand along the counter of the cosmetics department as they walked by it. "You know what my dad wants more than anything in the world?"

"Uh-uh."

"River access." Will halted and lifting a Boucheron perfume tester from the counter, sprayed some on the back of her hand. "Want some?" She cocked her head at Caprice.

"I'll try this one." Caprice sprayed a mist of Chanel Number Five onto her wrist, then warmed it with her breath. She held out her wrist, and Will sniffed it.

"Ooh, this is nice, too! But I like mine better."

They made for the escalator, and on the way they passed a young man who rolled his eyes and said, "Sheesh!" as he was subjected to the overpowering reek of their combined perfumes. They could barely wait till he was out of earshot before collapsing in giggles, and they were still chuckling when they reached the girls' department on the second floor.

As Caprice ran her gaze over the many racks of dresses, the child ducked under the nearest rack and disappeared. Caprice browsed but could see nothing special and was just about to give up when Will reappeared. Her cheeks were flushed, her eyes alight with excitement.

"Look!" She was carrying a hanger on which hung a pink velvet dress with a pink-piped white collar. "What do you think, Mrs. Kincaid?" Stepping to a three-way mirror, she held the dress in front of her and with her nose screwed up scrutinized the effect. "Will this be okay?"

Caprice hid a smile. The little girl had obviously forgotten her resolve to buy a dress that wasn't "way beautiful," a dress her father wouldn't notice! Gabe would have to be blind not to notice this one or to see how it suited his little girl.

"It's absolutely perfect. Let's find a changing room, make sure we get the right size. And then we'll get you some pretty socks and a pair of black patent shoes."

"Are we going to be spending an awful lot of money?" Suddenly doubtful, Will looked at the dress. "Dad always says money doesn't grow on trees."

"It's my treat," Caprice said.

"But...you're from Break Away..."

"I can afford to buy you an outfit. Truly I can. And delighted to do so!"

Will beamed at her. "I just love you, Mrs. Kincaid!" And then skipped joyfully away toward the fitting rooms.

As Caprice followed, her delight was suddenly overtaken by an overwhelming sadness. Will was such a dear little child, it was going to break her heart to leave her.

"Malcolm Lockhart's *dead?*"

Lou Anders nodded. "Yup."

"You're sure?"

"My wife went to a high school reunion back east on the weekend. She heard it there."

"So the old geezer's finally gone." Gabe fixed his gaze on the lawyer, who was eyeing him shrewdly from his swivel chair on the other side of his desk. "Well, I'd be a hypocrite if I said I was sorry."

"What I want to know, Gabe, is—if the riverside property goes up for sale, are you still interested in acquiring it?"

"Are you kidding?"

"It won't go cheap. Can you swing it?"

"Lou, I'll mortgage the resort and my very soul if I have to. I want that piece of land—and the river access that goes with it—so badly it damned well hurts!"

CHAPTER EIGHT

CAPRICE noticed, when she and Will met Gabe, that he had an air of coiled excitement about him that hadn't been there before. What had he and the lawyer talked about, she wondered? She itched to know but didn't want to pry.

He, however, had no qualms about asking Will what she had in her glossy fuchsia carrier bag.

"It's a secret, Dad. We can't tell you. Yet."

"Then I'll have to contain my curiosity, won't I!" Though his lips curved in a smile and his eyes crinkled at the corners, the eyes had a far-off look, as if he was thinking of something entirely different.

Caprice was certain he'd totally forgotten about the talk they'd had the night before regarding Mrs. Norton's visit. And he obviously had far more pressing matters on his mind than what his daughter was going to wear to a concert—unlike Will, to whom it had become of paramount importance.

The moment they got home, she whispered to Caprice, "I'm going to try on my dress again!" and scurried excitedly off to her bedroom. Caprice called after her, "I'll give you a shout when dinner's ready."

"Need any help, Caprice?" Gabe asked.

"Thanks, but I have everything organized. I cooked a casserole this morning. I'll heat it and then we'll eat."

"I have time to make a couple of phone calls?"

"Sure, go ahead."

"Thanks. So…give me a shout when dinner's ready? I'll be in my office."

Caprice had not only prepared a casserole that morning, she had made a blueberry pie.

She popped the casserole in the microwave oven, and by the time it was hot, she had cooked potatoes and broccoli and carrots and the kitchen was filled with a delicious savory aroma. She made custard for the pie, and then after setting the table, she went to round up Will.

She knocked on her door.

The door opened an inch. "Where's my dad?"

"In his office."

"Can you come in a minute?" The child ushered Caprice in and shut the door quickly again. She was wearing her new outfit, but she looked despondent.

"What's wrong?" Caprice asked. "You look just lovely!"

Will grimaced. "Except for my hair." She crossed to her dresser mirror, leaned toward it and ruffled her fingers through the raggedy strands. "It's so ugly!"

Tactfully, Caprice said, "Which hairdresser do you usually go to?"

"I don't." Will turned. "I always get my dad to cut it. But I don't get it cut very often."

Because she'd never wanted it to look nice. But now she did. And Caprice's heart went out to her. "What time does the concert start tomorrow night?"

"Seven."

"I'll pick you up right after school, take you to the farm and have Mark's mom fix your hair. How about that?"

"Oh, goody! Yes, please!"

"I'll phone the farm now." Caprice went to the door. "You'd better get back into your old clothes—you don't want your dad to see you all dressed up, not until tomorrow! What's Mark's number?"

Will recited it, and Caprice returned to the kitchen. She lifted the receiver to her ear and was about to dial when she heard Gabe's voice.

"So I may have river access soon and then I can expand my outfit—"

She put down the phone. She would call Merrily after dinner.

A few minutes later, Will came into the kitchen.

"Did you talk to Mark's mom?" she asked.

"I'm afraid the line was busy. I'll try again after we eat. Would you tell your dad that dinner's ready?"

While Caprice dished up the casserole, she found herself thinking idly about the snippet of conversation she'd overheard. Had Gabe found someone in the vicinity who was selling riverside property? It seemed that way...and it would explain the excitement that had tingled around him after he came from the lawyer's office.

She found it disappointing, though, that he hadn't shared his news with her.

After dinner, while Gabe took Fang out, Caprice called Merrily to set up Will's appointment.

And then she went to the lounge, where Will was diligently practicing her concert piece, "Chapel Bells."

Caprice went to a sofa and sat down to listen.

When Will had played the last note, Caprice got up and went to the piano. "That was perfect, Will. I'm so looking forward to tomorrow night."

"Me, too! Did you call Mark's mom yet?"

"Yes, we're to go there directly after school, and

she's going to give you a shampoo, styling and blow-dry.''

''I've never been to a real hairdresser!'' Will bubbled with anticipation. ''Is it fun?''

Caprice laughed and gave her a hug. ''It's one of the most fun things,'' she promised, ''that we women can do!''

After bringing Fang in, Gabe went to look for Caprice.

He found her in the lounge with Will. The two were standing by the piano, hugging and laughing about something.

When he called hi, they both whirled, then exchanged quick glances with each other before facing him with shuttered expressions.

''Hi,'' they responded in unison.

He vaguely recalled that Will had said something about a secret when he'd asked her in Cedarville what she had in her plastic bag—and she'd had that same shuttered look in her eyes then as she had now.

''Aha!'' he said. ''What have you two been up to?''

''It's nothing, Dad. Truly.'' Will bit her lip, but then a giggle erupted, and she couldn't quite stop it.

He raised his eyebrows and said, ''Well, I can see I'm not wanted around here!'' Lips twitching, he turned on his heel. ''I just came by to tell you I'll be in my office. I have a bit of correspondence to see to.''

As he walked out, he could hear Will's giggles, then the sound was smothered.

Her secret would undoubtedly be revealed in the full-ness of time, he reflected. Meanwhile, he did have a pile of paperwork to do, and once he got stuck into it, all thoughts of Will and her secrets vanished from his mind.

She popped by to say good-night to him before she

went to bed, and after she'd gone, he continued working. By the time he emerged from the office, it was after ten.

Caprice was busy in the kitchen, measuring baking ingredients into a yellow bowl. She looked up when he came in, and he saw that her cheeks were flushed, her nose dusted with flour. He wanted to haul her into his arms and kiss that flour away. But he wasn't about to act like a caveman. A more civilized approach was definitely called for.

Tell that to his hands, which ached to grab her. He slid them into the hip pockets of his jeans. "Aren't you finished in here? Look, I appreciated your offer to look after Will and me while I was sick, but I'm fine now. There's no need for you to be working—"

"It's not work, Gabe, I enjoy baking. And I especially enjoy doing this—I'm making a cake for tomorrow night." A strand of hair fell to her cheek, and she used her shoulder to brush it back. "I thought the three of us could have a little party when we come home from the concert."

She was like a Norman Rockwell portrait of a fifties mom. Doris Day. The girl next door turned perfect wife. *Wife?*

The word, which normally would have sent him running, dangled before him with the hypnotic appeal of a carrot to a donkey. Swiftly, he warned himself it could never be. Though Caprice Kincaid seemed to fit the part, she was a city girl, and city girls didn't settle in the country. At least, not for long. After the novelty wore off, they got bored; they got itchy feet. The plain fact of the matter was, they didn't belong here.

But was it possible, a sly and seductive voice whispered in his ear, that this city girl was different?

If only he knew her better.

"So if we leave here around six-thirty," she was saying, "we should be in plenty of time to get a good seat at the front of the hall?"

She was obviously speaking about the concert.

"Yeah," he said. "Six-thirty should do it." He pulled out a chair and sat at the table. He watched her for a while, as she measured sugar, milk and butter. Then, adopting a teasing tone, he said, "Caprice, we had a deal—in return for my telling you all about the Ryland-Lockhart family feud, you promised to tell me some of your deep dark secrets."

She was adding salt to the flour mixture, and he noticed that her hand gave a little jerk. Aha, he'd hit a nerve! Acting as if he hadn't noticed, he tilted his chair and grinned at her.

"So," he drawled, "where would you like to start?"

She added baking powder to the flour mixture, and scooped up a sifter before saying with a light shrug, "I don't know. You're the one who said I have secrets. My past is pretty uneventful. I was born, I went to school, I graduated from high school when I was seventeen—"

"Okay," he said. "Let's start from there. What did you do after you graduated?"

"I studied music. And I took some cooking classes. And then I got married."

"What did your ex-husband do?"

"He was a carpenter, worked for my dad."

"How have you been earning a living," he asked, "since your divorce? Do you get alimony?"

"I didn't want alimony." She finished sifting, and added hot milk and melted butter to a bowl of whisked eggs and sugar. "I just wanted him out of my life."

"Why? Or is this one of your secrets?"

"No, there's nothing to hide. I divorced him because I found out he wasn't the man I thought he was."

"He let you down?"

"He married me for…all the wrong reasons. And they had nothing to do with love."

He heard a faint tremor in her voice, so he directed his questions away from this obviously sensitive area. "Once you were on your own, how did you support yourself?"

"I worked for my father. Kept house for him, organized his schedules, entertained his clients, that kind of thing. It kept me busy."

"And now that he's gone…what do you plan to do?"

"I haven't really thought about it yet. I'll eventually sell the family home…but not yet. I want to hold onto the memories for a while. Maybe next year."

"When you do get around to looking for another job, you'll have no problem getting one. You're a fantastic cook. You could work in a kitchen somewhere—in a restaurant, or a fancy hotel, or even in a place like this."

As soon as he'd spoken the words, he was visited with a tantalizing picture of her in the big lodge kitchen at the height of the season. Or taking part in one of his wilderness hikes—cooking for his clients, and then at night lying with him on a blanket on some rugged mountain slope, staring at the stars, holding hands, talking about their dearest dreams—

He cleared his throat. "Or you could get a job teaching piano. Are you qualified for that?"

"Yes, I could teach piano." She folded the flour into the egg mixture, poured the batter into a cake tin, smoothed it with a knife and slid the cake into the oven.

When she faced him again, he said, with a smile, "So that's it? You really don't have any deep dark secrets?"

She transferred the dirty dishes to the dishwasher. "I think," she murmured, wiping the table, "that most of us have a secret or two deep down inside. I'm sure you have several that have never seen the light of day."

"No," he said. "I've told you all of mine." He gestured with open palms. "What you see is truly what you get. I'm not a great believer in secrets, Caprice. But whatever your secrets are, I'm sure that they don't reflect badly on you. I'm a pretty good judge of character, and I'd bet every penny I have that you're as honest as the day is long. I have to tell you, you wouldn't last a nanosecond here with me if you weren't, because if there's one thing I abhor above all others, it's deception. Lies and deception. In my book, those two are absolutely unforgivable."

That night, as Caprice lay in bed, miserable and unable to sleep, Gabe's words rang in her head.

And they still echoed there next morning as she looked at him over the breakfast table and felt as if her heart was breaking.

He was sitting back comfortably in his chair, drinking coffee, scanning the newspaper, occasionally reporting a piece of news to her.

His black hair was a stark contrast to the white T-shirt that stretched over his wide shoulders. The window behind him was open, and the gentle morning air drifted in, carrying the scent of his aftershave to her and making her yearn to run a tender hand over his smooth jaw.

She forced her attention away from him and looked at Will, who was eating the last crumbs of her scrambled eggs on toast. The child was unusually quiet. Was she perhaps wondering and worrying about her father's reaction to seeing her that evening in her pretty dress?

Caprice resolved to drive her to school and reassure her on the way.

She waited till the child had run off to brush her teeth before saying, "Gabe?"

The newspaper crackled as he held it aside. "Yeah?"

"I'll drive Will to school this morning. It'll be my last chance."

He quirked an eyebrow. "Last chance?"

She inhaled a deep, calming breath. She hadn't yet told him this was going to be her last day in the valley. What would his reaction be? "I'm leaving tomorrow."

"Oh, I see." He gave her an absent smile. "Sure, you drive her. But as to leaving—there's no rush, is there? Stay another week—at least till my clients arrive. I'll be tied up then, but in the meantime you're more than welcome to hang on here." His grin was lopsided. "I'm getting used to your cooking!"

Caprice only barely managed to bite back a gasp. But she felt as jolted as if he'd thrown a bucket of ice cubes in her face. It wasn't that she'd expected him to beg her to stay on in the valley...but she certainly hadn't expected this nonchalant response.

Was that all she meant to him—a provider of tasty meals? Disappointment poured through her, but it was immediately overtaken by sour resentment. How he had fooled her, with his talk of wanting to become more than friends. To him, after all, she had been just a toy to pick up and play with when he was bored!

She couldn't believe how gullible she'd been! She'd lost her heart to a man who cared nothing for it, or for her. You'd think she would have learned her lesson from Liam, her ex-husband. Apparently not.

"Thanks," she said, "but I've made up my mind."

Seemingly not noticing the stiffness in her voice, he

returned his attention to the paper. "Well, it's your decision, of course. I won't try to argue you out of it. But if you should change your mind—"

"Dad." Will addressed him from the doorway. "Ready?"

Caprice lifted her purse from the countertop. "I'm driving, Will. Do we have to pick up Mark?"

"Uh-huh!" Will ran to give her father a hug, then, grabbing Caprice's hand, pulled her to the door. "Bye, Dad," she called. "See you later!"

Caprice couldn't wait to get away. One more moment and she'd have lifted the frying pan and bashed it furiously on Gabe Ryland's handsome, arrogant head!

Gabe was pacing his office when he heard Caprice return.

He'd been pacing it for more than an hour and a half—with frequent trips to the window to glare out, his irritation surpassed only by his deep concern. Where the devil could the woman be? he'd asked himself over and over. Had she been in an accident? He'd even called the school, but was told that his daughter and Mark had been dropped off at the regular time and were safely in class.

When at last he heard the hum of an approaching vehicle engine, he strode to the window. And when he saw her Honda pulling in at the lodge steps, relief blotted out his irritation—but only momentarily. As he marched out of the room to meet her, his face was set in a dark scowl. She barely had the front door open when he exploded.

"What the hell took you so long?"

She did a double take. "Excuse me?"

"It doesn't take two hours to drive the kids to school. I've been worried sick, woman! Where the devil have you been?"

"I'm sorry." She moved past him. "I dropped by
Holly Cottage. I wanted to double-check that I'd
switched everything off. And then it was so lovely by
the river, I took a chair to the dock and just sat in the
sunshine for a while. I'll be spending the best part of
tomorrow either sitting in a car or a plane or hanging
around an airport so I—"

"Back up." Gabe stared at her bewilderedly. "Where
are you going tomorrow?"

She stared at him, looking as bewildered as he felt.
"I told you." She swung off her shoulder bag and set
it on the table. "I'm going home."

"Going *home?*" He repeated her words in a stunned
tone.

"Mm." She frowned. "I told you I was leaving."

"I thought you meant you were leaving the lodge! I
assumed you were going back to Holly Cottage!"

"Ah."

Her ah had a that-explains-it intonation. But explained
what? Then, with the impact of a thunderbolt, it dawned
on him. When she'd said earlier that she was leaving,
he'd acted as if it was no big deal, and he vaguely recalled a stiffness in her response. Now he knew why.
She'd been put out because he'd appeared not to care.
And he'd made some asinine remark about missing her
cooking.

Oh, dammit!

He had to let her know that her leaving was a big
deal.

"Caprice." He scratched a hand through his hair and
gave her a rueful smile. "We've been talking at cross-
purposes. I thought you were going to be staying on in
the valley. I thought you meant you were moving from
the lodge to Holly Cottage."

"No. That's not it. I'm going home."

"But why? You told me Break Away had given you carte blanche as to how long you could stay. Has that changed?"

She shook her head.

"Then...I don't understand your rush. You're certainly looking better than you were when you arrived here from the city, but another week of country air would do you a world of good. Stay, Caprice. Here, at the lodge. And it's not just your cooking I enjoy. You *know* that."

"I really appreciate the invitation, but... Well, it's just that I've sorted out everything that was jumbling my mind. It's time to go home, time to make a fresh start."

He could see she was adamant. And he felt a stab of panic. No way was he going to let her go. It might be better, though, if he pretended to accept her decision and seemed to be making the best of it.

He gave her an easy smile. "Okay. I'll miss you, though...so let's at least spend the rest of today together. I have to take a trip down the valley to an auction in Anstruther. In that letter from Alex, he forwarded a cutting about a couple of rafts for sale that I might be interested in." He could see her doubtful expression, so he added coaxingly, "I'd like the company."

She hesitated, and then she nodded. "Okay. But I need to tidy the kitchen first—"

"It's done."

"Then just give me a few minutes to tidy myself, get out of these old jeans. We'll be back, won't we, by three? I told Will I'd pick her up. We have a...couple of things to do before the recital."

She had that veiled look in her eyes again. She and Will were definitely up to something. But he knew he'd get nothing out of her; this was a woman who didn't give up her secrets easily. For the moment, however, he'd take what he got, which was the opportunity to spend time with her alone, time to work on her and persuade her that she really must stay at the lodge for at least another week.

"We'll be back in good time," he said. "Don't worry. Now go get yourself ready, and we'll hit the road!"

Accepting his invitation had not been a good idea.

Caprice sighed as she came out of the bathroom. Adding a day of memories to the memories she already had of Gabe was only laying up more pain for herself in the future. But she hadn't been able to resist. When he used that coaxing tone, she could deny him nothing.

If only she had never come to the valley.

If only he wasn't so darned attractive.

She bit her lip as she caught sight of herself in the dresser mirror. Her cheeks were flushed, and her eyes sparkled. What a fool she was. Wanting to look her best for a man she could never have, she'd not only changed into her favorite blouse and cream slacks, she'd applied mascara, ash-blue eyeshadow and a pink lipstick the exact same shade as her blouse. And not content with that, she'd finished with a subtle spritzing of scent at her pulse points.

It did occur to her, as she flicked her hair and put on her best silver earrings, that it was more than a little cruel to bait a line when she had no intention of letting the fish come close enough to have even one bite!

It wasn't till she went to the foyer and saw Gabe leaning casually against the reception desk that she realized, with a sharp pang of dismay, that if this particular fish decided to bite, she wouldn't be able to flip herself out of his reach. She was already hooked.

And he was already eating her with his eyes.

He pushed himself from the desk and came toward her.

She tensed, expecting a huskily spoken compliment, but he just said cheerily, "Ready?" and ushered her to the door.

They reached the little town of Anstruther at noon.

Gabe drove along the main street till they reached the auction hall. He parked the Range Rover, and as they walked to the building, he said, "The auction itself doesn't start till one, but we can view the lots, then we can go for a walk and have a bite of lunch somewhere before we come back."

The auction hall was a big barn of a place, brightly lit but dusty, with a planked floor and long tables spilling over with everything from jewelry to brass lamps to small electrical appliances. One wall was lined to the ceiling with furniture—tables, chairs, wardrobes—and against the opposite wall rolled carpets were stacked high.

The rafts—two of them—were at the far end of the building, in a corner by the stage.

Excusing himself, Gabe took off to look at them, while Caprice wandered up and down the aisles, pausing here and there to have a look at something that caught her eye and finally coming to a halt at a tray of jewelry.

Most of it, she soon discovered, was junk. But she had just unearthed a heart-shaped silver locket—promising though darkly tarnished—when Gabe materialized at her side.

"Are the rafts what you expected?" she asked.

"I'll bid for one. It's just what I need. There's a good chance I may be expanding my business, hiring another guide...." He looked at the locket in her hand. "You found something you like?"

His abrupt change of subject made her blink. It was clear he didn't want to talk about his business, but why? Once again she recalled what she'd overheard him say on the phone about the possibility of gaining river access. But even as she wondered why he didn't want to discuss the details with her, he took the locket from her, brushed it against his jeans and inspected it with interest.

"It's sterling silver," he murmured. "A beautiful piece."

"It *is* lovely, isn't it? Just needs cleaning."

He tried to click it open without success.

"Here," she offered, "let me."

With her thumbnail she pried it open.

Inside was a snap of a young couple, their faces ashine with happiness.

Looking at the doting couple in the photo made Caprice think of her father's photograph of Angela. He must have loved like this at one time, she reflected sadly, only to have suffered the anguish of losing the woman he loved and blaming himself for her death, bearing that burden for the rest of his life. As she thought of his pain, Caprice felt emotion well inside her.

Blinking back a tear, she dropped the locket into the tray and reached in her bag for a tissue.

Gabe frowned. "What's wrong? What's upset you?"

"Nothing," she said quickly, and hoped he'd believe her. "It's just...I'm allergic to dust," she fibbed. "And it's musty in here. Do you mind if we go outside now, take a walk along the river? I just need a breath of fresh air."

CHAPTER NINE

GABE seemed satisfied with her explanation.

Relieved, Caprice happily went along with his idea to buy deli sandwiches and take-out coffee and have an alfresco lunch in the town's picturesque riverside park.

The sun's rays were fierce, so they opted for a tree-shaded bench. And after they'd eaten, they stayed a while, enjoying the warmth of the day in companionable silence.

Eventually, Gabe said, "Time to get back." But as Caprice made to rise, he said, "No point in your coming, since the dust bothers you." He got up and tossed their garbage into a nearby container. "I shouldn't be too long. The rafts are number five in the catalogue."

She shaded her eyes with her hands as she looked at him. She could hardly protest, although she'd had a hankering to bid for the silver locket. Hiding her disappointment, she said, "I'll be here." And added, as he strode off, "Good luck!"

He came back half an hour later. And he was smiling.

"You got the raft?" she asked.

"Yup, and at a reasonable price."

"How are you going to get it home?"

"I've arranged for it to be delivered. So—" he pulled her to her feet "—we can be on our way."

They made their way to the Range Rover, and as Gabe drove the vehicle along the main street, she said, "We'll be back in time for me to pick up Will. Oh, by the way," she added in a deliberately offhand tone, "I'll be dropping Will off with Mark at the farmhouse. She's been invited there for dinner, and she'll be going on to the concert with Mark and his parents.''

"Oh, yeah?" He chuckled. ''Those two kids, sometimes I think they're joined at the hip.''

He didn't seem at all surprised at the arrangement, which had been Merrily's idea, when she'd heard that Will not only had a dress, she wanted a haircut.

"What fun!" she'd said. "Tell you what, Caprice, bring the dress with you when you pick the kids up after school. Will can have dinner here, and after I do her hair, I'll dress her up and she can come to the concert with us. We'll make sure her dad doesn't catch even a glimpse of her till she's actually up on the stage...and when he does, my goodness, his eyes are surely going to pop out of his head!''

Yes, thought Caprice as she stole a peek at Gabe, they surely would. She smiled at the prospect.

He glanced at her and said, "Ah, you're smiling. You're enjoying yourself? You're glad you played hooky?''

"Mm, it's been a lovely outing.''

"Good." He nodded, and contentedly fixed his attention on the road.

Caprice's gaze lingered on his rugged profile. And as she looked at the strong nose, the chiseled lips, the firm jaw, she felt an agonizing ache in her heart. Anyone seeing the two of them in the park might have thought them a long-married couple, well beyond the early feverish stages of wanting to jump into bed with each other at the drop of a hat. They would have been so wrong about that—at least in her case. Every time she looked at Gabe, she wanted to fall into his arms and make mad, passionate love with him.

But he no longer showed any signs of being roman-
tically interested in her. And she could trace this change
in his attitude to the moment she'd made it clear she was
leaving the valley for good the following day.

It was obvious he'd realized there was no point in
pursuing her when she wasn't going to be around for
much longer.

She should have been glad that his feelings for her
had been so shallow. It would surely make it easier tomorrow, for both of them, when she dropped her bomb-
shell.

But meanwhile, it provoked a feeling of despair.

Will and Mark were waiting when Caprice turned up at
the school.

"Did you bring my dress and stuff?" Will asked anxiously as she flung herself into the front seat.

"Mm." Caprice glanced at Mark as he jumped into
the back and slammed the door. "Hi, Mark."

"Hi, Mrs. Kincaid."

Will was as jumpy as a hyperactive flea. "You didn't
tell Dad the reason I'm going to the concert from Mark's
house is so he won't see me till I'm up on the stage?"

"No, I didn't tell him any of that." She pulled the
car away from the curb. "Don't worry."

Will expelled a noisy sigh. "I can't help it, Mrs.
Kincaid. Part of me is so-o-o looking forward to the
concert...but the other part of me is so-o-o worried
about what my dad will say, that I feel as if I might
explode."

That evening, as Caprice strolled with Gabe across the
car park to the school, she recalled Will's words and
hoped the child was coping with her anxieties. At any

rate, the waiting would soon be over, and Caprice was confident that Gabe would be thrilled with the new Will.

He was edging a fingertip irritably under the collar of his dress shirt. "I tell you, Caprice, I hate wearing a tie—I'd like to wrap this one around the neck of the guy who invented them and choke him with it!"

Caprice chuckled, but as she glanced at him, she found her throat turning dry. He looked absolutely devastating in his dark suit, white shirt and a hunter green tie that intensified the green of his eyes.

Earlier, when they'd met in the lodge sitting room, she'd felt her heart melt at sight of him. Now proximity to his tall powerful body and exposure to his potent male chemistry combined to melt not only her heart but every single feminine cell she possessed.

He blew out a sigh. "Hot, isn't it!"

"You can say that again!" she said with a fervor that was not directed at the weather.

"And sultry," he added. "Look at those dark clouds to the west. I guess a storm's on the way."

"Let's hope," she said lightly, "that it doesn't arrive till after the concert."

He dropped his hand from her elbow as they reached the entrance, and she was thankful, because when he was touching her, she could think of nothing else. Once in the hall, she was distracted by all the people who wanted to chat with Gabe. He was obviously very popular.

Eventually they worked their way through the throng, and when Gabe spotted two empty seats in the center of the fourth row, he said, "Let's grab those."

As they squeezed their way along the row, with people calling greetings to Gabe from all sides, Caprice murmured teasingly, "Is there anyone here you *don't* know?"

"Nope. And they're all eaten up with curiosity about you. They haven't seen me with a woman for three years…and when I do have one on my arm, she's a smasher!"

Caprice sank into her seat, but not before he'd seen her blush. He dropped down beside her, and leaning close, murmured, "They're probably wondering what you're doing with an old geezer like me."

As his shoulder wedged against hers, he noticed that she tried to edge away. But where could she go? If she moved another inch she'd be sliding onto Jennie McCall's lap. No, he mused smugly, she was stuck with him. For the duration of the recital, she was stuck with him, and he meant to take full advantage of that fact. During their outing to Anstruther, he'd let her have her own space. He'd been friendly, but nothing more. His strategy had been to throw her off guard…

And make his move tonight.

He felt a surge of excitement—the thrill of the chase—as he loosened his tie. "It's even hotter here than it is outside, isn't it!" And it was. Not the slightest breeze drifted in through the open windows and doors. A ceiling fan whirred, but for all the good it did, the school board might as well have saved the electricity.

He saw that Caprice was using her program to fan herself.

"I'm on the school board," he murmured, "and I've been fighting for the past couple of years to get air-conditioning in here. Maybe after tonight, I'll have more support."

While he was talking, he oh-so-casually slid an arm over the back of her chair. And smirked as the rhythmic beat of her fan faltered. It quickly picked up again, but pressing his advantage, he went on.

"What *are* you doing here with an old geezer like me, Mrs. Kincaid?" He slipped his hand under her hair, subtly caressing her nape with his fingertips.

She stiffened but turned her gray eyes on him steadily. "I'm here because I promised your daughter I'd come, and when I make promises I try to keep them."

"Admirable." He toyed with the clasp of her necklace, and savored the silky texture of her hair as it rippled over his knuckles. "And when," he murmured as the master of ceremonies took the stage, "are you going to let me in on whatever secret it is that you and my daughter have been sharing?"

"Very soon."

The MC tested the microphone, and as he did, Caprice leaned toward Gabe and put her lips to his ear. He thought, for a crazy moment, that she was going to kiss him, but even as his breath caught, she whispered, "Would you please remove your hand from my neck? This is a children's school, Mr. Ryland, not some sleazy nightclub!"

He laughed. "Yes, ma'am!" His reply was drowned out as the MC started speaking. He did as he was told, and then leaned back in his seat, ready to relax and enjoy the show.

A few moments later, the concert began with a number by the senior choir, the boys dressed in shirts and pants, the girls in dresses or skirts and blouses. An attractive bunch.

Mrs. Norton, who was accompanying the choir, sat at a piano to the left of the stage. Gabe half-closed his eyes and imagined his daughter there, tousle-haired, grinning, her T-shirt probably half untucked from her jeans, the jeans clean but faded, maybe even ragged at the hem.

With a bit of luck, though, Mark's mom would have made sure she at least washed her face.

He'd given up hoping his tomboy daughter would ever emerge from her chrysalis and become the butterfly he knew she could be. Perhaps she needed a woman's touch for that, a mother's touch. Maybe he should have married again, provided her with a stepmother. But he hadn't, and he carried that guilt around with him. Besides, Will seemed to like things just the way they were.

And what the heck, he loved the kid no matter what. And if she was the only one here who didn't dress up, he would never let her know how disappointed he was.

All he wanted was for her to be happy.

Caprice felt her excitement mount as the concert progressed.

And not only because of Gabe's closeness, although that was very distracting and his renewed advances quite puzzling. She couldn't wait to see Will. As a trio of kindergarten boys finished an energetic tap dance to rousing applause, she sat up straighter.

Will was next.

She hadn't seen the child since dropping her off at Mark's. She'd offered to wait while Will had her hair cut, in case the child needed input as to style, but Will had said, "No, thanks, Mrs. Kincaid. I know *exactly* how I want it done!" And clutching the bag containing her toothbrush and her concert outfit, she'd raced off after Mark.

How would she look, with her raggedy hair tamed?

And how would Gabe react when he saw her?

He hadn't asked what his daughter would be wearing, had shown not a whit of interest in the matter. But surely during the past hour he must have noticed that all the little girls on stage were wearing dresses or skirts?

Then again, perhaps not.

Or perhaps he didn't care.

The boys had exited the stage. The audience hushed as they awaited the next performance.

Caprice inhaled a deep breath. Closed her eyes. And when she opened them, Will was stepping across the stage.

Oh, my. Caprice stared at her, absolutely bedazzled. Mark's mom had cut Will's hair quite short, and it was a sassy starburst of honey-gold. She was beautiful. Even more beautiful than Caprice could have imagined.

As the child walked tentatively to the microphone, Caprice heard a soft murmur from the audience, and from nearby heard someone whisper, "Isn't she *darling?* And what a pretty pink dress!"

Caprice sneaked an excited look at Gabe to see how he was reacting. What she saw made her blood run cold. And then red hot. The man was yawning! He was actually yawning! Slouched in his seat, his eyes on his daughter, he looked as if he was ready to fall asleep.

Openmouthed, she stared at him. He tapped his program against his knee. *Can't wait till this is over.* He didn't need to say the words; she could read them in his actions.

Of all the reactions she might have expected from him, indifference was certainly not one of them.

The man was a monster!

As she fought to contain her fury, Will's voice came shyly over the microphone.

"My name is Will Ryland," the child said, in little more than a whisper. "And the piece I'm going to play on the piano is—"

Gabe jolted upright. And knocked his knees against the back of the seat in front of him. Sending it sliding, with a grating of chair legs on the parquet floor.

Silence followed.

In that startled silence, Caprice—and everyone else in the hall—heard Gabe boom, in a tone of utter astonishment and disbelief, *"Will?"*

Then Caprice knew the reason for his indifference. Gabe Ryland hadn't recognized his own daughter. Relief flowed through her like balm on a wound. Holding her breath, she looked at the stage.

Will was peering at the audience. "Dad?"

Gabe got to his feet. "Is that you, Will?"

Caprice saw Will bite her lip. Then, wrinkling her nose, she said in an apprehensive little voice, "Yes, Dad. This is me."

Gabe scratched a hand through his hair, tufting it up in spikes, and his mouth slanted in a crooked smile. "Honey," he said. "You look beautiful!"

Will beamed at him as if he'd just handed her the moon. And to a round of applause and gales of laughter from the audience—along with a boisterous, "Way to go, Gabe!" from some man at the back—Will ran to the piano.

Afterward, although Will assured her she'd played her piece without making any mistakes, Caprice couldn't have told her one thing about her performance. Her attention was focused solely on Gabe, and on her happiness that he had reacted in an even more gratifying way than she could possibly have imagined.

And she told him so, during the intermission.

"You were *great*, Gabe. I was so *proud* of you."

His eyes twinkled. "Made a bloody fool of myself."

"I think it's a moment Will's never going to forget."

They had stepped outside in the hopes of escaping the oppressive heat in the hall, but though darkness had fallen, there wasn't the slightest breeze to cool the air. The night was ominously still and ominously quiet.

Except for a distant rumble of thunder.

"That storm's coming closer," Gabe murmured. "We'll be lucky to get home before it breaks."

In the end they didn't. The rain started to patter down as parents left the hall and went to the back to pick up their children.

Gabe and Caprice found Will sitting impatiently on a chair by the door. When she saw them, she jumped up and ran to them. She had eyes only for her dad.

He swung her up and gave her a warm hug. "Honey," he said, "you were fantastic. Unbelievable!"

As he dropped her to the floor, she said anxiously, "And you truly like me when I look pretty?" She looked at him, wide-eyed, waiting.

"Like you?" He ran a hand over her silky blond cap. "You'll never know just how much!"

With a blissful sigh, she looked at Caprice. "You're a really smart person, Mrs. Kincaid."

Gabe cocked a questioning eyebrow in Caprice's direction, but she just said, "Will can explain everything to you later. In the meantime, we should be getting on our way. It's going to be a wild night."

By the time they got home, the rain was lashing down. After parking, Gabe loped into the lodge to get an umbrella, and when he came back, he sheltered Caprice and Will under it as he escorted them quickly to the door. He was about to close it behind them when Fang scampered into the foyer, darted between Gabe's legs and shot outside.

Gabe said, "I'll wait here till he's ready to come in. He won't stay out long in this weather!"

Caprice and Will went to the kitchen.

"How about a cup of hot chocolate with our cake?" Caprice asked.

"Mm, goody." Will perched on a chair. "Wasn't this the funnest night? And I just love my hair like this. I can't wait till I'm old enough to wear earrings!"

The milk was simmering in the pan by the time Gabe walked into the kitchen, Fang at his heels. The dog moseyed over to Will. He sniffed her shoes, ran his nose up her ankles to her calves, snuffled the hem of her dress.

Will chuckled. "Fang thinks I must be somebody else," she said. "He doesn't recognize me."

"Your dad didn't, either," Caprice said, smiling as she spooned cocoa into three mugs and stirred in the hot milk.

"It's not every day—" Gabe leaned lazily against the countertop "—that we get to see Cinderella at the ball! And you, sweetheart, had better get yourself off to bed the minute you've finished your cocoa and cake—we don't want to see you turn into a pumpkin."

"Oh, Dad—" she laughed "—that wouldn't happen till midnight! Besides, my name's not Cinderella." Slipping off her chair, she skipped to the middle of the kitchen and spun around and around till the skirt of her dress flew out in a pink blur. Eventually she lost her balance and fell against Gabe, who caught her. As she looked at him, her eyes became serious. "Can I ask you something, Dad?"

"Fire away."

"From now on—" her voice had a trace of anxiety "—I don't want to be called Will. My name's Willow.

It's a pretty name.'' She asked in a rush, ''Don't you think it's a pretty name, Dad?''

''I should think I do! After all, I was the one who chose it!''

''You did?''

''Darn right I did!''

The child's eyes shone like polished gems. ''This,'' she said, giving her father a ferocious hug, ''has been far and away the happiest day of my life.''

Later, when Caprice was tucking Willow into bed for the night, the child said sleepily, ''You were right, Mrs. Kincaid. My dad loves me, no matter what.''

''I've been thinking, Will—''

''Willow!''

''Sorry. I've been thinking, Willow, that you ought to tell your dad about your play place in the attic. He should really know that you go up there sometimes— just in case he's ever looking for you, for something important, and he can't find you.''

''You're right.'' Willow yawned. ''I dozed off up there once and he was looking everywhere for me. But if I tell him, will he be mad at me for opening up the trunk and using all my grandma's clothes and stuff?''

Caprice smoothed a reassuring hand over the child's soft hair. ''He's not going to be mad at you. Trust me.''

''Okay, I'll tell him tomorrow.'' Willow's eyelids were drooping.

''Will you tell your dad, too, why you've been keeping it all a secret?''

''Keeping what a secret?'' Gabe's amused voice came from the doorway.

Caprice jumped. But Willow was too close to sleep to be startled. Drowsily, she whispered, for Caprice's ears alone, "You tell Dad the part about me seeing him crying. I'll tell him the rest...about the attic... tomorrow."

Caprice switched off the bedside lamp and tiptoed from the room. Gabe stood aside to let her pass, then closed the door behind them.

"What was all that about?" he asked as they walked to the sitting room.

"Will—Willow—has had a few secrets she's been keeping from you over the years. She's going to spill most of them tomorrow...except for one. And she wants me to tell you that one. Tonight."

"Kids and their little secrets! So...what has Cinderella been up to? Did she break a vase or fail a math test or—"

"Gabe." Caprice touched his arm. "This is serious."

He stopped short. And instantly became serious. Eyes narrowed sharply, he said, "What?"

"Could we have a drink first? I think," she added with a dry laugh, "that we're both going to need one."

"Why would you need one?"

She crossed to the hearth and turned to look at him. "For Dutch courage. This isn't going to be easy, Gabe. For either of us. What I'm going to tell you...you may find it deeply upsetting."

His response was to stare at her for a long moment, then stride from the room. "Hang on," he said over his shoulder, "I'll get the drinks from the kitchen."

When he returned, he was carrying a glass of Scotch in one hand, a glass of white wine in the other. He gave her the wine, and she took a seat in an armchair by the hearth.

Gabe remained standing. Glass in hand, he faced her. "Right." His expression was grim. "Shoot."

She took a few sips of wine and balanced the glass on her knee. "It would help," she said quietly, "if you would tell me what happened the night your wife walked out on you. From your...point of view."

He looked stunned. For a moment, she thought he was going to deny her request. But he didn't. "What do you want to know?"

"What did you do that night?"

"Do?" His laugh was bitter. "I sat here, in that very chair—" he waved his glass at her seat "—where you're sitting now, and I got as drunk as the proverbial skunk." He took a gulp of Scotch from his glass. "Shocked?"

"Of course not. That was your way of deadening the pain." She braced herself for what she was going to say next. "And you *were* in pain. I know...because you cried."

He stiffened. "You're guessing, of course." He hardened his gaze when she shook her head. "What are you, then, some kind of psychic?"

"Your daughter saw you."

"Will?" He shook his head violently. "Oh, no, you have to be wrong—"

"She saw you, Gabe." Caprice tightened her fingers around the wineglass. "She couldn't sleep. She was missing her mom. She wanted a hug. She went looking for you, and—"

"Oh, God. She didn't—"

"She heard you in here and she peeked in. She saw you...and an empty whiskey bottle. She said you were crying, and—"

"Why did she never *tell* me?"

"This is where it gets difficult." Caprice wondered

how she could make this easier for him but knew there
was no way, no way other than to spill out the whole
truth. "She heard you saying that you hated beautiful
women, and that you'd never again love anyone who
was beautiful—"

Gabe made a hoarse little sound.

"—and your daughter made up her mind, there and
then, that she would spend the rest of her life making
herself plain so you would never stop loving her."

In the silence that followed, all she could hear was
her own breathing. Gabe seemed frozen, as if turned to
granite.

Finally, when she was ready to break the silence in
desperation, he said, in a voice that she barely recognized, "Dear God, that poor kid." Blindly, he set his
glass on the mantelpiece. "What in the name of heaven
have I done to her?"

Caprice put down her glass, rose swiftly and closed
the space between them. Putting her arms around him,
she said comfortingly, "You weren't to know, Gabe.
And everything's all right now. I talked with Willow
yesterday, told her you would love her no matter what
she looked like or how she was dressed—"

"But all these years! Feeling insecure like that—"

"Oh, no, Gabe, she hasn't ever felt insecure. She always knew you loved her. Her only mistake was in
thinking it was a conditional love. She was confident that
as long as she was a scruffy little tomboy, she had nothing to worry about. Certainly she stifled her natural
yearning for pretty clothes, but no harm has come to her
because of that. She's a happy child, Gabe." Suddenly
she realized she still had her arms around him. She withdrew them and stepped back. "You've done a tremen-

dous job of bringing her up. You should be proud of yourself, not beating yourself up!''

''For some time now I've felt that she was keeping a secret from me, but I'd never have guessed in a million years that it was this.'' He clenched his fists against his thighs. ''You said earlier that she had other secrets.''

''You don't have to worry. This time, it's no big deal. At least, I don't think it is. But she does want to tell you herself. She has something to show you, and when she does, be patient—it's something very special to her. And if you react negatively…well, it'll spoil her enjoyment in something that has given her a lot of pleasure. She's going to tell you tomorrow.''

''Tomorrow.'' He gazed at her moodily. ''You're leaving tomorrow. And how do you think I'm going to manage without you? Look what you've achieved in the short time you've been here! Willow has opened up like a flower. She's really taken to you, Caprice. She's going to miss you like the devil.''

''I'm going to miss her, too.'' She smiled wistfully. ''I fell in love with her the moment I set eyes on her— the first morning I was here. I bumped into her when I went for a walk before breakfast. Of course she didn't know you'd given me a bed for the night, and she told me I'd better keep off Lockhart property if I didn't want to be looking down the barrel of her dad's shotgun!''

Gabe laughed, and it was wonderful to see him relaxed again. But even as she savored the moment, she felt her mood sober. She *would* miss Willow…but even more than that, she would miss Gabe. She'd fallen head over heels in love with him. It was going to break her heart to leave.

If only she could stay.

''Stay.''

She blinked, wondering for a moment if she'd spoken aloud. But of course she hadn't. It was Gabe speaking.

He pulled her into his arms. "I need you, Caprice. I never thought I'd say this to a woman again, but...I can't even imagine how lonely this place is going to be without you. How lonely *I'm* going to be without you." He wove a hand through her hair and cupped her head with his fingers. "You mean so much to me."

His kiss was the sweetest, and at the same time the most devastating, she had ever experienced. His lips were soft but firm, velvety smooth but demanding. He kissed her till she was clinging helplessly to his shoulders, her fingers digging into his flesh, her pulses scrambling.

He smelled of hot skin and need; he tasted of whiskey and chocolate. His breathing was shallow, his intent river-deep. And his body was as hard as tempered steel. She kissed him back till they both were afire.

And he whispered, against her heated cheek, "Come to bed with me, my love...."

Then, and only then, did she struggle free.

Breathless, flushed, she stepped back from him. "It's no use, Gabe." Her voice caught on his name. "Making love will only make parting more difficult than it's already going to be. I *have* to go. Nothing you say or do will make me change my mind."

He didn't try to stop her as she walked away, but she could feel his unhappiness. It was matched by her own.

Tomorrow, though, he would feel differently about her. Before she left—which she would do, right after breakfast—she had to tell him the truth about who she was.

She had never dreaded anything more.

CHAPTER TEN

CAPRICE woke early next morning.

Her mood was somber, her body knotted with tension.

She decided to go for a walk in the hope that fresh air and a bit of exercise might alleviate her nervous dread.

After showering, she dressed in a black turtleneck sweater and black jeans, topping the outfit with a fleecy vest in a black and silver geometric pattern. With her hair gathered in a black velvet scrunchie and her feet clad in a pair of black leather ankle boots, she crept from her room and made her way outside.

The morning was misty and cool; the damp air clung to her hair and dewed her cheeks. Slipping her hands into her vest pockets, she walked down the grassy slope to the fence that divided the Ryland property from hers.

She stopped for a moment, gazing out over the trees. Because of the mist, she couldn't see the chimney pots, but she knew where they would be.

She sighed. It seemed like an eon since the night she'd arrived when—city slicker that she was—she'd fled because of a bird. But what might have happened if that bird hadn't found its way down the chimney? She'd have settled at Holly Cottage that night and she might never have met Gabe Ryland. But she would have met his daughter, because Willow, assuming her to be from Break Away, would have come down to offer Fang and friendship.

She closed her eyes as the pain of leaving the child

swept over her. And following fast on its heels came the unbearable pain of leaving Gabe.

If only...

"Hey!"

She spun around. And her heart lurched as she saw the man of her thoughts striding toward her out of the mist. He was wearing a blue checked shirt and jeans, and he looked as if he'd come straight out of bed. His hair was tousled, his jaw unshaved. And his green eyes were fixed on her with a hard look that sent apprehension skittering through her.

He halted two steps from her. And confrontation emanated from him in waves.

She resisted a panicky urge to hunch over and wrap her arms around her body in self-protection. Instead, she squared her shoulders and said, "Hi, were you looking for me?"

"I heard you go out. I wanted to talk to you where there was no chance of Will hearing—"

"Willow," she reminded him automatically.

He bulldozed over the interruption. "—because I didn't sleep one wink last night and I've come to a decision. There is no way I'm letting you leave here today until you give me a commitment that we'll see each other again." He slashed a hand in the air to stop her as she would have spoken. "You can't just walk into my life and then walk out again as if nothing has happened. Something *has* happened, dammit, and you can't just ignore it!"

She felt a sizzle of alarm as she saw the blaze of anger in his eyes. "Gabe, my mind is made up. I told you. I'm leaving today."

He fumbled in the breast pocket of his shirt and held something out. "This is for you. The words...they'll tell you better than any of mine exactly how I feel about you.''

He had bought her the silver locket. He had cleaned it, and he had polished it, and it gleamed more richly than any silver she had ever seen. And now that it was shiny clean, she could see that it was engraved with three words. Heaven is love.

She felt her heart break.

''I...can't take this. I—'' She faltered, then forced herself to go on. ''I have something to tell you. I was going to tell you just before I left. But...it's better I tell you when Willow's not around. And it will explain...everything.'' She held out the locket.

After a brief hesitation, Gabe took it and folded his hand around it. He'd play along with her—for the moment. But whatever it was she was going to say, he wouldn't let it keep her from him. He'd sensed all along that she had secrets, but nothing could affect the way he felt about her.

Nothing.

When he had walked out of the mist and had seen her by the fence, he'd felt his love for her well up till he almost drowned in it. She was so very beautiful, but it wasn't her looks he'd fallen in love with, it was the woman herself. He'd fallen for her sweetness, her sincerity, her warmth, her compassion. And he wanted her to be his wife. He would stop at nothing to make it happen.

''Go on,'' he said. ''But whatever you have to tell me won't make a whit of difference to the way I feel about you. I promise you that. I love you, Caprice—now and forever.''

Her eyes had taken on a haunted look. ''Gabe, just

listen. And please…please don't interrupt while I'm speaking.''

''Go ahead.''

She hugged her arms around herself. ''I've told you already that my father died recently. What I didn't tell you…'' She bit the edge of her lip. ''After he died, I found two things locked in a drawer. One was a photo of a young woman, someone I didn't recognize. The other was my father's birth certificate.''

Gabe wondered, with a touch of impatience, where this was leading and what it could possibly have to do with him. He indicated, however, that she should go on.

''My father and I had always been very close, and I had never known him to lie to me. So when I looked at the birth certificate and saw that he'd been born somewhere other than he'd led me to believe, I was… distressed. But after I got over the shock, I wanted to find out why he'd deceived me. So I traveled to his birthplace to try to get some answers.''

Gabe said, ''And did you have any luck?''

''I found my answers.'' Her eyelids flickered. ''Here.''

''Are you saying your father was born in Hidden Valley?''

''He was born in Cedarville General Hospital. And—'' she turned toward the fence ''—he lived down there.'' She raised an arm and pointed.

''In Holly Cottage?'' He frowned. ''That must have been before my time. The Lockharts have owned that property for as long as I can remember. Was your father a friend of the family? Did he perhaps board with them? Or—''

She turned back, and the haunted look in her eyes stopped him dead.

"What?" Frustrated, he threw up his hands. "I don't get it, Caprice."

"The woman in the snap was called Angela." Her voice was so rough it scraped his nerves. "I know now—I've learned since coming here—that she was your mother."

He stared at her, unable to take in what he was hearing. Unable to make any sense of it.

Then, as he saw her eyes fill with anguished tears, he knew—knew even before she spoke again—exactly what she was going to say.

And fury was already exploding inside him with a savagery that almost felled him when she whispered, in a voice so low he could barely hear it, "Malcolm Lockhart was my father."

Caprice saw Gabe stumble. Saw his features contort with emotion. With rage, and with pain.

The rage she could bear; the pain she could not.

With a sob, she brushed past him and fled up the grassy slope and over the crest of the hill to the lodge.

By the time she got inside, she could barely see for her tears.

She had packed her things the night before. She hurried into the bathroom, swept up her toiletries, dropped them into her toilet bag, stepped quickly into the bedroom and shoved everything into her overnight bag. She was about to hoist her case from the carpet when she heard a sound in the doorway.

With a gasp of alarm, she looked up. But instead of seeing Gabe, she saw his daughter. Willow was still half asleep, and she was rubbing her eyes with both hands. Walking forward, she said drowsily, "Where are you going?"

Caprice took in a deep breath and forced herself to slow down. She crouched to the child's level and held her gently by the shoulders.

"It's time for me to leave. I was going to say goodbye after breakfast but…I'm leaving a little earlier than I expected."

Willow yawned. "When will you be back?"

"Sweetie…I won't be coming back."

The child gaped at her, suddenly totally awake. "You're not coming *back?*"

Her incredulity hit Caprice like a blow. "Willow, you've known all along that I'd be leaving—"

"Yes, I knew that, all the Lockhart ladies leave in the end—but you're *different*. I thought you'd be coming *back!*" Her skinny little figure looked slighter than ever in a thin blue flannel nightshirt that barely reached her knees, but when Caprice reached out to take her in her arms, Willow shrank away from her as if she couldn't bear to be touched. "You shouldn't have stayed long enough to let us like you so much if you weren't planning on coming back. You should have *told* us you didn't like us!"

"Willow, I do like you! I like you and your dad more than I can say—"

"You're just like my mom! She didn't like us, either. And she didn't care that we both loved her—she still left! Oh, I just *hate* you!"

She spun away, shot out of the room and into her own, slamming the door shut behind her.

The sound echoed in Caprice's head as she remained crouched for an endless moment.

Then wearily, oh, so wearily, she straightened. Hitching the straps of her handbag and her overnight bag over her shoulder, she picked up her case. And after one last look around to make sure she'd left nothing behind, she walked out of Ryland's lodge.

The mist was clearing, but of Gabe there was no sign.

Less than a minute later, she was driving along the highway, her chest as heavy as if it had been filled with lead.

Clutching the steering wheel with white-knuckled hands, she tried to console herself by saying aloud that at least she had found, in the valley, what she had come looking for.

But that did nothing to cheer her up. She had not only found the answers to her questions, she had also found love.

But though she was bringing those answers with her now, she had lost and left something she could never recover.

Her heart.

In the middle of the night, Willow woke to the sound of Fang whimpering.

Switching on her bedside lamp, she expected to see him in his usual spot, at the foot of her bed. Instead, she saw him lying on the carpet, facing the door, his nose between his paws. He turned doleful eyes to her. And that was when she heard a thumping sound from along the passage.

Clambering out of bed, she padded past Fang. She crept along the hallway and stopped at the sitting room. The door was ajar. And when she peeked around it, her heart started to go boom-boom-boom real quick, and she whispered, "Hell!" It popped out so fast that even though she clamped her hand over her mouth she was too late to stop it. But she was too worried to care.

Her dad was stomping around and saying some *truly*

bad words that made her toes curl. She had never seen him so angry. His face was whiter than white, and his eyes were flashing like her grandmother's fake emerald necklace when the summer sun caught it through the attic skylight. But he wasn't drunk. Not like that night when her mother ran away. There wasn't even one single glass or bottle in the whole room. And that, she understood, was a blessing.

If only she knew what she should do. One half of her wanted to sneak back to bed and hide under the covers. But the other half, the braver half, said no. She had to tell her dad that even if Caprice didn't like him, she did. Because that might just make him feel better. And the only thing she wanted in the world was for him to be happy.

Taking a deep breath, she gave the door a shove and walked into the room. "Dad?"

He whirled. She saw him swallow real hard, and then he raked both hands through his hair, and when he dropped them again, his hair stood up in spiky tufts on top. He looked at her, kind of dazed, and then he heaved a great sigh and said, "Honey, did I waken you?"

She walked over to him. "Fang was crying. So I got up to see why."

He took her hand and led her to an armchair. Sitting down, he hoisted her onto his knee and put his arms around her. "I couldn't sleep. I was just letting off steam."

"'Cause Mrs. Kincaid took off and she isn't coming back."

Gabe looked into his child's earnest eyes and bit back the bitter words burning his gut, burning to be spoken. To express them would be pure selfishness. Willow didn't need to hear a tirade directed at the woman who

had used the two of them to solve the mystery of her
father's past. The woman who had lied and deceived and
manipulated and—

"Dad?"

"You're right, Willow. I'm upset because of Mrs.
Kincaid."

"I'm upset, too, Dad. I truly thought she liked us both.
But she didn't. And of all the Lockhart ladies, I thought
she was the nicest—" She stopped, her eyes wide with
dismay, and pressed a hand over her mouth.

Gabe tilted his head, regarded her warily. "What do
you mean? You didn't know any of the other—"

"I did, Dad." She grimaced and fiddled nervously
with a fold of her nightshirt. "I know you're going to
be real mad at me for this, but I s'pose I'd better tell
you."

Gabe listened, with growing astonishment, as his
daughter began by relating how she'd gone down to the
log house in search of Fang and finished by telling him
about the pictures on the fridge and how she'd gone
down early one morning to get them back.

"So…" She faltered as she came to the end of her
story. "Are you mad at me, Dad? For breaking your rule
and going on Lockhart land?"

"Honey, it's not okay for you to break my
rules…except when you talk about it with me first and
we come to some agreement. But what you did, taking
Fang down to these ladies, was a good thing. And a kind
thing. I'm proud of you for doing it. I don't think you'll
need to go down there again, though."

"Why not?"

"I have a feeling that Holly Cottage will be going up
for sale soon, and then there'll be no more Lockhart
ladies for you to visit. So let's forget about the past.

Let's make a fresh start.'' He dropped a kiss on her brow. ''It's time for us to get back into the old routine.''

''Dad, there's just one more thing.''

He cocked his eyebrow.

''Mrs. Kincaid said I should tell you, in case you're ever looking for me and can't find me.'' She wrinkled her nose. ''I play in the attic sometimes. There's a trunk of old clothes and some other neat stuff, and I dress up. I think the clothes belonged to my grandma.''

A shadowy memory flitted into Gabe's mind—a memory of his father flinging all his mother's clothes and jewelry into an old trunk after she walked out, and hauling it into the attic. When he'd come down, he'd said to Gabe, ''I don't want you ever going up there, son. I want you to forget your mother ever existed. We're better off without her. Beautiful women—take it from me, boy, they're nothing but trouble. When your time comes to get married, look for somebody plain. That way, you can always be sure that the only bed she sleeps in will be your own!''

He hadn't taken that advice. And his father had been proved right. Twice. He hadn't got as far as marrying Caprice Kincaid…but he'd wanted to. And she'd turned out to be as genuine as plated silver—all gleam and polish on the surface, but inside worth spit.

''Dad?'' Willow nudged his arm. ''Is it okay, about the clothes? Can I still play in the attic?''

''Sure. But just tell me first, before you go up there. That way, I'll know where to find you.''

She yawned and curled her arms around his neck. ''I love you, Dad.'' She kissed him, then she slid off his knee. ''I think I'll go to bed now. Are you going to be okay?'' She looked at him anxiously.

''Yeah,'' he said, in a reassuring voice totally at odds

with the way he was feeling. ''Yeah, honey. I'm going to be okay.'' And pushing himself to his feet, he walked her to her room.

Fang was asleep on the covers at the foot of the bed.

Gabe tucked his daughter in, kissed her and put out the light. It had been a day like no other, he thought.

And he was glad it was at an end.

''I have a ten o'clock appointment,'' Caprice said to the receptionist. ''With Mr. Duggan.''

The young woman smiled. ''Mr. Duggan's waiting for you, Mrs. Kincaid. Please come with me.''

The lawyer's office was on the twentieth floor of Chicago's prestigious Beechley Tower III building, and as the receptionist ushered Caprice through the doorway, she saw Michael Duggan standing by the window that overlooked the lake.

He came forward as the receptionist pulled the door shut silently behind her.

''Mrs. Kincaid.'' He held out his hand. ''Good to see you.''

They shook hands, he gestured toward a burgundy leather sofa, and she sat down. He took a seat across from her on the other side of a rosewood coffee table.

''Well,'' he said heartily, ''how did your trip go? Did you find out why your father kept his birthplace a secret?''

Caprice had already decided exactly what she was going to tell the lawyer and exactly what she was going to keep back. ''His family had been involved in a nasty feud with another local family. He left the valley on a sour note—and I think he just wanted to forget that part of his past.''

"He must have known you'd eventually find the birth certificate."

"Maybe he didn't look that far ahead. Or if he did, he probably figured it wouldn't matter anymore." She sensed that the lawyer wanted to continue probing, so she abruptly changed the subject. "Why I wanted to see you this morning is...I want to sell the Hidden Valley property."

"Sure. I'll get right onto it."

"Just one thing."

He waited.

"Before you list it on the open market, I'd like you to contact the man who owns the adjoining property. I met Mr. Ryland, and he indicated he'd be interested in buying. Give him first option. And...I don't want to go into details, Michael...but we—the Lockharts—owe Mr. Ryland and his family something. Something we can never really repay. But give him a deal." She rose to her feet. "Just make sure you don't offer him such a good deal that he suspects we're doing him a favor. Gabe Ryland is a very independent man."

Gabe stood on the crest of the hill, his gaze stark as he stared over the property below. Lockhart property.

In his hand was the letter he'd received an hour ago from a lawyer in Chicago. The Lockhart lawyer. *Her* lawyer.

He'd been right when he'd figured she'd sell the house. And the land that went with it. What need would she have for it when she intended never to come back?

In his hand he held the answer to a dream he had cherished for longer than he could remember. At last that dream was within his grasp. He didn't need to call the bank to find out if he could swing the deal. He knew he could. The price was reasonable. More than reasonable.

Slowly, he walked down the slope till he came to the fence. And there he halted. He could hear the birds warbling in the trees, could smell the spicy scent of the long grass and wildflowers. And he could hear, as if she was beside him, Caprice Kincaid's voice—as sweetly alluring as that of a siren.

They wouldn't be secrets anymore, if I were to share them with you! But I might share one or two of them, if you share one or two of yours. You could start by telling me what you have against the Lockharts!

He gritted his teeth. And crunched the lawyer's letter, with its sweetly alluring offer, into a tight, hard ball. Savagely, he hurled it over the fence, where the wind picked it up and carried it away, to disappear into the forest.

"Your Mr. Ryland turned down the chance to buy the Hidden Valley property." Michael Duggan's voice came to Caprice over her cell phone as she was driving in her white Jaguar to meet an old family friend for lunch. "He sent a fax this morning."

"What did it say?" Caprice held her breath.

The lawyer replied in a tone tinged with curiosity. "He said he wouldn't touch the property with a barge pole. Mrs. Kincaid, what's going on?"

Caprice braked sharply as she almost rear-ended the city bus in front of her. Gathering herself, she said, "It's personal, Michael."

"Shall I list it now?"

She picked up speed as the bus turned onto a side street. "Let's leave it for the time being. I'm not sure what I'll do with it now. I'll have to think about it. Is there anything else, Michael?''

"Chad called re the opening ceremonies for Marsden House. Your father was to have made a speech, and Chad asked if you'd be willing to take his place. It's not till October, but Chad wants to get everything settled now.''

"Sure. I'll do it.''

After she clicked off her phone, Caprice realized her hands were clammy, and she was shaking. She pulled the Jaguar to the side of the road the first chance she got.

She leaned her head on her forearms, on the steering wheel. Her eyes were dry of tears. She had shed so many, since coming back from the valley, she didn't think she had any left. But inside, in her heart, she wept. For Gabe. And for the pain he must be feeling.

It must be tearing him in two that his dream had finally been within his reach, but because she was the one who was offering it, he was unable, because of his pride, to accept it.

And now she had to face up to the fact that she really would never see him again. She had cherished a secret hope that if he'd agreed to purchase the property, it might open the way to their being in communication again. To start building a relationship again. But her hopes had been in vain. He would never forgive her.

She might as well get used to the idea and get on with the rest of her life.

Alone.

CHAPTER ELEVEN

GABE had never known a summer to pass so slowly.

For the first time ever, he found the days dragging, and he felt little enthusiasm for his work. But he showed nothing of his dark moods to the groups he took into the wilderness. He challenged them and he praised them, and they responded by giving their best. By the campfire, under the night skies, he would smile at their eager talk and jovial camaraderie. But later, when everyone else had fallen asleep, he would lie alone, staring at the stars, and feel his heart as empty as the vast spaces above.

By the time October rolled around he was weary and looking forward to the end of the season; looking forward to the two-week break he'd take before the winter skiing.

Willow seemed happy enough, but she never spoke about Caprice Kincaid. And her blossoming interest in beautifying herself had withered as swiftly as had her admiration for the woman who had nurtured it in the first place.

He tried not to think of Malcolm Lockhart's daughter, and for the most part he succeeded. But once in a long while, she slipped past his guard and sneaked in to play havoc with his rigidly disciplined thoughts. Those occasions, however, were rare, and after each one he fortified the sturdy ramparts he'd erected around his heart.

On a Saturday afternoon toward the end of October, he was in the lounge chatting to a group of white-water rafters who were leaving next day when he saw Willow beckon to him from the door. Excusing himself, he walked over to her.

"Dad," she said, "can I go up to the attic and play?"

"Sure. Actually, I'll come with you. I've been meaning to check the lighting, make sure everything's safe."

They went to the third floor together, then Willow ran on ahead. As he clambered up the narrow winding stairs leading to the attic, he could hear her slippered feet pitter-pattering across the planked floor.

Dusk was falling and only a hazy light filtered into the long room from a solitary skylight. Beneath the skylight he saw a table and a rocking chair. And by the chair was an old steamer trunk.

Willow already had the lid open.

As he moved to join her, he could see neat piles of clothing. Vividly colored. Silky. Feminine. And hats and purses and belts. Then, as Willow folded back a drift of wispy scarves, he saw a nest of jewelry. He must certainly have seen his mother wearing some of these items, but they moved no veils in his mind, exposed no long-ago images.

He felt surprise and a sense of relief that he could look at her things and feel only a vague curiosity. He had, it seemed, wholly recovered from the wounds inflicted by her cruel rejection. He could only pray that one day Willow, too, would become immune to the hurt *her* mother had caused her.

"You have lots of fun with that stuff, mm?" he asked absently as he switched on the light, checked the cord, found everything okay.

"Oh, I do, Dad. I truly do!"

He wandered around, poking here and there, but found nothing to concern him. His footsteps echoed hollowly as he walked back to sit down on the rocking chair.

Resting his forearms on his knees, he leaned forward and looked at his daughter. "How come," he said conversationally, "you like to dress up when you're in the attic but you don't want to get all dressed up when you're downstairs or at school?"

Her attention seemed focused on a scarlet and orange striped scarf she was looping around her neck, but when she spoke, he detected a faint tremor in her voice.

"This was my secret place," she said, "before *she* ever came. This was *before*. It's the *after* stuff I don't want to do. Up here, I can just be pretty for myself. Not for other people."

He knew, of course, who the "she" was. But Caprice Kincaid was one person he did *not* want to discuss.

"You know something, Willow Ryland?"

"What, Dad?" She looked at him innocently.

"You, sweetheart, are the best thing that ever happened to me. I don't know what I'd ever do without you!"

"You'll never have to, Dad. I'm not going anywhere."

He felt the smarting of tears, and to hide them, he leaned over and scooped up a charcoal gray bolero that Willow had slung over the lid of the trunk.

"I don't ever play with that," she said with a disdainful sniff. "I don't like the color." She picked up a blouse of fuchsia satin and put it on. Next she extricated a pair of high-heeled pumps, slid her feet into them and started teetering over the floor, giggling with every precarious step.

Gabe chuckled and was about to put the bolero down when a sheet of folded paper slid from an inside pocket and sailed under his chair.

He picked it up. Unfolding it, he saw it was a letter,

written in a strong hand with black ink that had faded with time.

The letter was to his mother. It began, "My dearest Angela…"

He read the letter from beginning to end without glancing to the foot of the page to identify the sender. But by the time he got there, he already knew who the sender was. He didn't need to read the signature or the final message, although he did read them, all the same.

And he read them aloud, though he could barely hear himself speak for the blood that pounded in his ears.

"I will come for you tonight. Be waiting. Always your devoted servant, Malcolm Lockhart."

"One more shot, please, Mrs. Kincaid."

"Yeah, darlin'. Just one more?"

"Please. This one's for the—"

"Over here, look over here…"

Caprice adjusted her black cashmere wrap, and pausing at the top of the steps, turned to face the jostling photographers. Flashbulbs popped, making her blink.

"Fantastic dress!" A reporter shoved a microphone at her. "Versace?"

She allowed him a faint smile before turning away. Tucking her hand into the crook of Michael Duggan's arm, she walked with him through the open doorway into Marsden House.

"There," Michael said. "That wasn't so bad, was it?"

"At least," she responded dryly, "they're not allowed inside! And I don't imagine they'll hang around till the fund-raiser's over. After all, it's not the event of the season."

"No, but there are a lot of important people here.

Your father counted many of the rich and famous as his friends.''

The foyer was packed with guests, the babble of their conversation interspersed with bursts of laughter and the occasional clink of ice against glass from the bar temporarily set up against one wall. Friends who noticed Caprice greeted her with enthusiasm, and she spoke to each one before moving on.

When she and Michael at last made it to the bar area, she said, "It's hot in here, isn't it?"

"Let me take your wrap." Michael slid the feather-light wrap from her shoulders and handed it to an attendant. "So, what would you like to drink?"

"A glass of Chardonnay. Thanks." As she spoke, Caprice caught a glimpse of her reflection in the mirror behind the bar. Her dress was indeed a Versace—strapless black velvet with jet beading—and she had bought it for this function. Her face, she noticed, was as pale as her shoulders and still had that strained look she'd had when she returned from Hidden Valley. Fighting a wave of unhappiness as memories flooded in, she ran a palm over her upswept hair before turning to accept her glass of wine.

"After dinner," Michael said, "there'll be several speeches. The mayor will speak first. You'll be last, after Madeleine Bronson. You said you'd made notes?"

"I have them here." She held up her jet-beaded evening bag and gave a rueful laugh. "In the event that I get stage fright, I'll just read them."

"You'll be fine. You can do anything you set your mind to, Mrs. Kincaid. You are, after all, your father's daughter."

In many ways she was, Caprice thought sadly. But in one crucial respect she was not. Of all the qualities a person could possess, she regarded integrity as the finest. Her father, to her unutterable regret, had lacked it.

She knew, in her heart, that she did not.

After Gabe read Malcolm Lockhart's letter and as soon as the poleaxing shock and horror had lost their initial intensity, he grimly acknowledged what he had to do.

He had to talk to Caprice Kincaid. And he had to do it face-to-face. There was no other way. He had to tell her what he had learned, and he had to be with her when he did.

He was many things, but he was not a coward.

So he had stayed up half the night talking with Alex Tremaine and reorganizing their schedule. The incoming clients were rookie hikers, and Alex was more than capable of leading them on their four-day trip.

He had tracked down Caprice's home address by finding Malcolm Lockhart's name in the phone book. And in the morning, he talked with Willow. All he told her was that he had to go to the city, and he'd call her.

After breakfast, he drove her to school, and from there he drove to Seattle, where he got the first available seat on a flight to Chicago. On arrival at O'Hare, he hailed a cab and directed the cabbie to take him to Lockhart House.

By the time he got there, his nerves were strung to breaking point. And when he saw the house, it was a wonder they didn't snap. He wasn't sure what he'd expected, but it certainly wasn't a magnificent white granite mansion set in acres of grounds. Floodlit on this October night, it was a spectacle that stole his breath away. Caprice lived here? He still felt disorientated when he rang the front doorbell.

A maid answered. Dressed in black with a crisp white

apron, she ran a narrowed gaze over his espresso leather bomber jacket and jeans.

"The tradesmen's entrance," she announced with a superior sniff, "is around the back."

"I'm not a tradesman. I'm here on urgent personal business. I need to see Mrs. Kincaid."

"Mrs. Kincaid is not at home."

Disappointment curdled through him. "When will she be back?"

"I don't know." She sounded impatient.

He shoved his hands into his jacket pockets and scowled. "Dammit, this is important. Can I come in and wait?"

She looked scandalized. "It would be more than my job's worth!" She made to close the door.

He stopped it with his foot. "Look, I'm…a friend of Mrs. Kincaid's. She stayed at my home in May, when she was out west."

He saw her hesitate. "Really?"

He placed a hand over his heart. "On my grand-mother's grave."

"Well…" She squeezed the word out. And then said reluctantly, "You can't come in…but I'll tell you where you can find her. She's gone out with her lawyer, Mr. Duggan, to a function at Marsden House, on Whittaker Road." Again she made to close the door. Again he stopped her.

"One more favor," he said. "Could you call me a cab?"

The cab arrived within ten minutes, and it took another thirty to get to Marsden House, which turned out to be a brick building that looked as if it might, at one time, have been a small hotel.

It was lit up like a Christmas tree.

Gabe paid the cabbie and walked slowly across the forecourt, which was jam-packed with Porsches, Beemers, Jags, Mercedes, Ferraris...

A flight of steps led to the entrance. Standing on the top step, to one side, was a red-haired young man wearing a tux.

He slanted a grin at Gabe. "A bit late, aren't you? You've missed dinner." He waved his cigarette toward the double doors. "Speeches are already started."

"I'm just here to...deliver something." Gabe pushed open the door and went inside.

The foyer was large, and deserted except for an attendant sitting reading behind a cloakroom counter and two men dismantling a temporary bar. They paid him no attention.

From behind a pair of swing doors he heard someone speaking, the voice amplified by a microphone. As he stepped across the carpeted floor, one of the doors opened and a woman came out. When she saw him, she held the door open. He nodded his thanks and slipped past her. As the door swung shut, he found himself at the back of a darkened banquet hall, with a brightly lit head table at the far end.

After his eyes had adjusted he could see that the hall was packed with tables, eight guests to a table. The men were in tuxes, the women in glittery evening dress. He reckoned there must be around three hundred guests in all. How the devil was he going to find Caprice in this crowd?

He stood against the wall, and as he did, the man at the microphone sat down after introducing a tall, silver-haired woman by the name of Madeleine Bronson.

While Ms. Bronson spoke, Gabe scanned the gathering intently for Caprice, but with no luck.

He returned his attention to the head table. And the speaker.

"...for whom this occasion must bring mixed emotions," she was saying, in a rich, cultured voice. "Sadness, because her father cannot be here tonight, but joy in the knowledge that his many friends continue to give full support to his endeavors and have so generously provided the funds necessary to run Marsden House as he intended it to be run when he donated it to the community, as a refuge for women in need. Malcolm Lockhart was a man with a vision. And here, to keep that vision alive, is his daughter. Ladies and gentlemen, will you please join me in giving a big hand to Caprice Kincaid!"

Stunned, Gabe stared at the speaker. Caprice's father had given this building to charity? And Caprice herself...she was among those at the head table?

Feeling as if he'd been sucker-punched, he sliced his gaze over the group and felt his heart fly to his throat when he saw a blond, stunningly beautiful young woman rise elegantly to her feet and walk to the microphone.

Just as he hadn't recognized Will at her concert, for a moment he hardly recognized Caprice. She was wearing a fabulous jet-black dress, off the shoulder, sleek-fitting, ankle-length. Her hair was upswept in a starkly sophisticated style. At her throat and her ears sparkled diamonds, so brilliant, so exquisite they stole his breath away.

If he'd been able to speak, he'd have said only one word: *Wow!* She looked, for all the world, like a princess.

And it hit him, all at once and with a sickening thump, how out of place he was here.

Gabe Ryland was rough and ready, a country boy.

Caprice Kincaid was chic and polished, a city girl.

And she was as graceful and as suited to this city milieu as a swan gliding over a mirror-smooth lake.

"Ladies and gentlemen." Her smile was disarming, her manner poised. "My father was, first and foremost, a family man. But he did have other interests. Other facets of his life that held him in thrall. One was his work, and making a deal." Chuckles from the audience. "Another was sailing, despite his complaint that the hobby was like pouring money into a bottomless pit." More chuckles. "And a third," she added with a smile, "was spending time with his friends, throwing parties at Lockhart House. But for my dad, his fourth and last interest was—well, it meant more to him, I think, than all the others put together—helping women in need." Applause rippled around the banquet hall. She waited for it to die down before she went on quietly. "We shall probably never know why my father had such an intense desire to care for suffering women. But what we do know is that his compassion was genuine and without compare. Ladies and gentlemen, I am proud this evening to stand here and on his behalf thank you all, from the bottom of my heart, for ensuring the success of Malcolm Lockhart's final and most treasured project, the Marsden House for Women."

She resumed her seat to a standing ovation.

And Gabe knew, with a feeling of leaden hopelessness, that this woman was way, way out of his league.

They were from two different worlds.

He acknowledged now what he hadn't admitted to himself before. He hadn't come to Chicago because he owed it to her to talk to her face-to-face; he hadn't come because not to do so would have been cowardly. He'd come all this way because, like a lovesick teenager, he'd had a romantic fantasy that after she read the letter, she'd fall into his arms and say, "Now there's nothing to keep us apart."

He smiled bitterly.

Nothing to keep them apart? Only her wealth, her position, her lifestyle. What did he have to offer her? A rustic resort in the boonies and a man who'd never owned a tux or a Porsche...never had and never would. And more important, would never want to. He must have been crazy, coming here. He felt like a fish gasping its last in the desert.

They were still cheering.

Someone switched on the lights.

Urgently, he pushed open the door and slipped out to the foyer. He had to get away. He didn't want to embarrass her, and he would, if he approached her. Battered leather jacket and jeans wouldn't cut it with this glitzy crowd.

People spilled into the foyer behind him. Wanting to run, he suddenly froze. The letter. He must get it to her. And without delay. Though she'd looked radiant while she gave her speech, under the surface her joy must surely be tainted by the belief that her father was an adulterer. He couldn't let her go on thinking that for one moment longer than necessary.

He darted a searching glance around the throng of people in the foyer and saw the red-haired man who had been smoking outside when he arrived. He was alone.

Gabe wove his way over to him.

"Excuse me," he said. "I have a letter for Mrs.

Kincaid. This is an imposition, I know, but…could you do me a very great favor and pass it on to her?''

"No problem." But even as the man put out his hand, he said, "Hey, there's Michael Duggan, her lawyer. That heavyset guy with the beard, over by the cloakroom. Why don't you pass it to him? He and Mrs. Kincaid arrived together. He'll no doubt be driving her home."

"Thanks," Gabe said. "Will do."

He caught Michael Duggan as he walked from the cloakroom carrying a wrap. The lawyer raised his eyebrows as Gabe grabbed his arm, but he said, pleasantly enough, "What can I do for you?"

Gabe had sealed the letter in an envelope before leaving home. He took it from the inside pocket of his leather jacket. "Mr. Duggan, my name's Gabe Ryland. Mrs. Kincaid and I met when she came to Hidden Valley earlier this year. Could you see that she gets this letter?"

"Gabe Ryland?" The lawyer's eyes took on a wary expression. "Aren't you the man who turned down the chance to buy the Lockhart property?"

Gabe shifted his feet restlessly. "Yeah, that was me."

"You've come all the way from Hidden Valley? Don't you want to deliver the letter yourself?"

Gabe noticed people looking at him curiously. He felt a surge of anger—not at them, but at himself. Anger at his foolishness in coming here. "Look," he muttered. "I've got to go. I have to get to the airport. Will you just promise me that Caprice will get that letter tonight?"

"Of course. But are you sure you don't want to—"

Gabe pushed his way through the crowd, and a few moments later, he was striding away from the building and onto the street. He walked till he found a cab.

And an hour later, he was at the airport.

*   *   *

"Thanks again for bringing me home." Caprice smiled at Michael Duggan as she escorted him from her living room to her front door. "And it was kind of you to come in and sit with me while I unwound. The evening went well, but I found it exhausting."

"You did well, Mrs. Kincaid...but you do look tired."

"Maybe I just need another holiday," she said lightly.

He made a tsking sound. "That reminds me...." He reached into the pocket of his tux. "I have a letter for you." Pulling it out, he handed it to her. "I meant to give it to you earlier but it slipped my mind."

She turned the envelope over in her hand. Nothing was written on it. "Where did you get it, Michael?"

"When I went out to the foyer to get your wrap, I was waylaid by a stranger—striking dark-haired fellow, outdoors type." He chuckled wryly. "Made the rest of us men look like store-window mannequins in our penguin outfits!"

Caprice's brow gathered in a frown. "A stranger? Did he say who he was?" She ran a fingernail along the flap of the envelope, and it easily slipped open.

"Yes, he introduced himself right off the bat. Turned out he was Gabe Ryland, the self-same guy who turned down the chance to buy your property in Hidden Valley."

Caprice waited till the lawyer left before she looked at the letter in its envelope.

She didn't take it out right away.

First, she poured herself a glass of wine. Then she carried the wine and the letter to the fireside and sank into one of the armchairs flanking the hearth. She placed the envelope carefully on the glass coffee table, then sank into her chair again.

Slowly, she sipped the wine. Sip after sip. Taking her time. And all the while staring at the white envelope. Wondering what the letter would say.

Would it be filled with venom? Venom that had intensified till he could contain it no longer but had been forced to spew it all out, put it down on paper and send it to her?

No, not even send it to her. He had flown more than halfway across the country to deliver it.

But at the last moment, he had drawn back; had given it to her lawyer instead.

Why? Because he'd been afraid of his own rage?

She drained the last drops from her wineglass. She couldn't put the moment off any longer.

Setting down the glass, she picked up the envelope and tugged the letter out.

She stared at it for a moment, taken aback. It wasn't written to her, after all. It was a letter written to Gabe's mother, and her heart gave an erratic lurch when she recognized her father's strong hand.

Hardly breathing, she started to read.

My dearest Angela,

What you told me today has distressed me deeply. I have hardly been able to bear your unhappiness over the past many months, but now, like you, I fear for your life. Caleb's jealousy, unfounded though it is and has always been, has made him unstable. You have done your best to convince him that you have never loved anyone but him, but he is blind to reason. And by threatening you with a gun, he has finally gone too far. Yes, my dear friend, I will willingly drive you to

Seattle, where you can find shelter at this safe house you have found. Leaving little Gabe behind will be the hardest thing you have ever done, but it would be even harder on the boy to rip him from his home, and from the father he adores.

I will come for you tonight. Be waiting.

Always your devoted servant,

Malcolm Lockhart

Caprice was shaking by the time she reached the end of the letter. It took several moments for the import of it to sink in. When it did, she pressed her fingertips to her lips and sent up a fervent prayer of thanks. Her father had not, after all, been an adulterer. The knowledge was like sunshine in her heart. She hugged this new truth to her—and shed several tears as she thought about how her father had tried to help Gabe's mother.

And on the heels of that thought came an understanding of why her father had devoted so much of his time, energy and money to the care of women in need. He had never, ever forgotten his dear friend Angela, and everything he had done had been in memory of her.

And then her thoughts turned to Gabe, who must recently have found this letter.

How devastating for him to learn that the father he'd loved had driven his mother away, and that in the final analysis Caleb Ryland had been indirectly responsible for his wife's death. If he hadn't driven Angela away, she wouldn't have been speeding along the highway to her tragic destiny in Malcolm Lockhart's car.

Gabe had let his hatred of Malcolm Lockhart spread a dark shadow over his life. That shadow was lifted. But for some reason, Gabe had decided not to approach

Caprice. He had come all the way to Chicago, so surely he must have meant to give her the letter himself.

But he had turned away at the very last minute.

And she thought she knew why.

CHAPTER TWELVE

FANG heard it first.

Gabe was waiting at the top of the lodge steps for the mutt to do his bedtime business and emerge from the forest when the animal gave a sharp warning bark.

As the sound faded, Gabe heard the purr of a fast-approaching vehicle. Seconds later, he saw the glare of headlights, and a car glided into the clearing.

Tensing, he drew his hands from the pockets of his jeans. Strangers in the night. Nowadays, one couldn't be too careful....

As the car pulled to a halt a few yards from the lodge steps, Fang rocketed over to it, barking wildly while dancing around it in a frenzy of excitement.

"Fang!" Gabe called. "Come here!"

Still yelping shrilly, the dog obeyed, hopping up the steps to take his stance beside his master.

Gabe snapped his fingers. "Quiet!"

After a low protesting growl, Fang became silent.

The powerful light above the lodge's entrance beamed onto the car. It was a white, low-slung Jaguar. And only one person was in it. Warily, Gabe watched the driver climb out.

But at sight of the familiar petite figure, he blinked in disbelief. And was dizzied by a feeling of déjà vu as the woman paused, her hands cupped at her brow to shield her eyes from the light before stepping confidently forward.

She stopped at the foot of the stairs, and with her face

174

shadowed by her hands she looked at him. "I know it's late—" her voice was husky and threaded with humor "—but can you give shelter to a weary traveler?"

Caprice.

Joy flashed through him, and he thought his heart might explode. But hard reality immediately plunged his exultation into a bucket of icy water. This was a mistake. Her coming back was a mistake. It would never work; he and Caprice Kincaid were from two different worlds. And he had walked away from hers without a backward glance, although he couldn't deny that the two weeks since he'd returned from Chicago had been the most miserable he'd ever known.

"Gabe?"

He stifled a frustrated oath. Why couldn't she have left things be? Why drag them both through this pain again? But he couldn't send her on her way without giving some reason for rejecting her. She deserved that.

"Sorry," he said. "It was just a...shock, seeing you." He stepped down to meet her. "Come in, we need to talk."

Fang bounded down the steps and excitedly nosed her, his tail wagging like mad. She bent to pat him. "Hey," she said softly, "nice to see you, too!"

"That's some car you've got there." Gabe ran his gaze over the Jag.

She straightened. "It was a present from my father on my twenty-fifth birthday."

Her tone was casual and held no hint of the apology he often heard in the voices of rich folk when they talked to hoi polloi. He was glad of that, because he found such apology offensive. It implied that he must envy their wealth, which he did not. "You drove here from Chicago?"

"I like to have my own wheels." Her eyes locked with his. "Unlike last time, this isn't just a trip. I plan on staying." Her eyes, usually the soft gray of a kitten's, had a steely glint that said, "Don't mess with *me*, buster!"

"You're going to live at Holly Cottage?"

"No. I'm going to live here, at the lodge. With you."

His joy escaped and soared again. Dammit, he was having a tough time trying to control it. Trying to damp it down, to stomp on it, to kick it to pieces. This would not work, he told himself grimly. This could not work. It was impossible. The very fact that she jaunted around in a Jag, for Pete's sake, that must have cost more than he cleared in a good season—

"Just a sec." She sashayed to the Jag and from the trunk hoisted an overnight bag. Her hair spilled forward in a stream of liquid gold as she leaned over…and the memory of its silk and scent had him aching to haul her into his arms and kiss her till her knees buckled.

She flicked the blond swath back and rejoined him.

"It's frosty, isn't it?" She looked at the crystal-clear sky, its deep indigo velvet sparkled with myriad tiny, perfect stars. "I wouldn't be surprised," she added, with a friendly smile, "if it snows tonight."

She was Miss Cool as a Cucumber. Totally in charge of the situation.

But he was not about to let her call the shots. He had his own agenda.

Gripping her elbow, he ushered her up the steps and into the foyer.

Fang took off immediately for Willow's bedroom.

Caprice dropped her overnight bag, slipped off her ankle-length navy boots, opened the hall closet and tossed the boots inside. Making herself at home.

Making a point.

"You know what?" She peeked at him as she hopped on one foot while adjusting the white sock on the other. "I'd just love a cup of tea! Shall we go into the kitchen?"

Without waiting for an answer, she padded off.

He followed, unable to keep his eyes from her splash of bright hair, so starkly pale against the navy of her blazer, and her sexy little behind and her long, long legs—legs that could make even her faded baby-blue jeans look elegant.

He wanted her so badly it hurt.

This was going to be the most difficult thing he'd ever done. How the heck was he going to convince her that she had to leave when he wasn't even sure he could keep his hands off her?

She had the kettle on before he'd even had time to draw breath. And then she moved competently around, taking out mugs, cream from the fridge, cookies from a tin. And all the while she hummed, as if their being together in his home was the most natural thing in the world.

And all the while, he watched, rehearsing in his mind exactly what he was going to say. And hoping that the ashamed tone he planned to use would be convincing.

He waited till they were seated at the maple table, two mugs of tea steaming in front of them, before he spoke.

First he cleared his throat. And then he set his palms on the table. Flatly. Firmly.

"Caprice." His voice came out exactly as he wanted it to. "You shouldn't have come. This is very embarrassing, but I don't think there's any way to say it without hurting you. And I don't want to beat around the bush—"

"Gabe," she said airily, "that's *exactly* what you're doing. Why don't you just...spit it out?"

He exhaled heavily. "Okay," he said. "Here goes. Caprice, what I felt for you...when you were here before...it was a...well, I guess what it was was just a...temporary infatuation."

"Really?" She quirked one perfectly arched eyebrow. And he thought he saw her lips lift at one corner. In amusement.

"Yes. Just...infatuation. Although," he hastened to add, "I know I led you to believe it was...more."

"More?"

"I feel really badly about this." He shifted uncomfortably in his seat. "Yeah, more. I think I led you to believe I'd, um, fallen in...love with you." This was more agonizing than he'd thought possible.

"Yes," she murmured. "That is what you led me to believe. And I can't remember if I ever told you I felt the same way, at least not in so many words. But I do, Gabe. I do love you." Her laugh was seductive, intimate. "Well, I wouldn't have come here to propose to you if I didn't!"

He thought he would choke. But his response had just the right amount of chagrin he'd aimed for. "Hell, Caprice, you make me feel like a heel. I had no idea that you'd taken me seriously—"

"Oh, I took you seriously, Gabe." She poured cream into her tea, stirred it lightly. And then picking a lemon cookie from the plate, nibbled a corner. "Mm," she murmured, her eyes widening in appreciation. "Did your cook make these? I must get the recipe, they're delicious." She cocked her head. "Sorry, Gabe, what were we saying? Oh, yes. We were talking about marriage—"

"No!" He sounded as if he were strangling. He swal-

lowed, tried to calm himself. "We were talking—*I* was
talking—about this…misunderstanding…and I take full
responsibility. I didn't make myself clear—"

"Oh, but you did." She pushed back her chair and
got to her feet. She walked around the table, and with a
feeling of panic, he got up, too, and backed away from
her. "You made yourself very clear. One thing does surprise me, though."

"And what's that?" he asked with a feeling of despair.

"I *expected* that you'd try to get rid of me, and I came
here prepared for it…but I thought the excuse you'd use
was that I'm a city girl. And city girls don't stay. At
least, in your experience."

She came close, and he found he was up against the
wall.

"I'm staying, Gabe. I'm not like your ex-wife. I won't
tell you I'll grow to like country living. I don't have to,
because I already love it." He flinched as she wound
her arms around his neck and looked at him with her
big gray eyes. Eyes that had lost their steely glint and
become misty with emotion. "Do you believe that?
Please tell me you do."

How could he not? What reason would she have to
lie? "Yes," he muttered…and wished she wouldn't arch
against him. She was driving him crazy. Crazy with
longing. "That I do believe. But I don't want you to
stay because—"

"Here's how I see it, Gabe. You fell in love with me,
then when I told you I was Malcolm Lockhart's daughter
you thought you hated me. You felt you *had* to hate me.
Then you found the letter—I want to hear about
that…later—and you came after me because you no
longer had reason to hate my father and you felt free to

let yourself love me. But then—'' she reached up and kissed his jaw ''—you found out that I had money—''

"That has nothing to do with—"

''—so you took off.'' She shook her head chidingly. "Gabe, sweetheart, I hadn't taken you for a coward!''

He gritted his teeth and tried not to succumb to her tantalizing closeness and intoxicating scent. "You've got it wrong,'' he lied vehemently. "I took off because I realized you weren't the same person—"

"You know something, Gabe Ryland? You're right.'' She ran a fingertip over his upper lip, and perspiration dribbled down his lower back. "I'm *not* the same person you believed me to be, but the only real difference is I have money. And I'm not about to apologize for that! It's a fact of life, and I've accepted it. And I'm not about to give it all away in some grand gesture. That's not what my father would have wanted. He would have wanted me to continue with his charity work, and that is exactly what I plan to do. So the problem, as I see it, is…are you man enough to accept me as I am, wealth and all?''

He felt his mind spin, his thoughts twist in a wretched turmoil. No, he wasn't man enough. He couldn't handle it. As a husband, he wanted to financially support his wife. He didn't want to feel like a…like a bloody gigolo!!

He grasped her hands and pulled them down. And stepped away from her. He faced her from a yard away. And looked her straight in the eye.

"No," he said. "It's not my style."

He had expected to see tears spring to her eyes. Tears of hurt. Maybe even anger. What was that old saying? Hell hath no fury like a woman scorned.

But what he saw in her eyes was disappointment.

"I was wrong about you, Gabe." She pulled her blazer around her, carefully fastened the buttons. "You *can't* handle it." She murmured a sound that was faintly mocking. "You told me once that more than anything in the world, you liked a challenge. You seemed to take pride in it. And here I toss down the gauntlet, and you can't even pick it up." Her smile chilled him. "You say I'm not the person you thought I was. That makes two of us, Gabe. You're certainly not the man I believed you to be. Sure, my money might have caused problems along the way, and it's too bad that you don't have the guts to confront them. To work with me to solve them. It's ironic," she said with an edge of bitterness. "My ex-husband married me for my money, but you won't marry me because of it!"

She spun away from him and made for the door. "Don't see me out, Gabe." Her back was stiff. Stiff as her voice. "I can find my own way."

Like a man who was drowning, he saw his life flash before him. Not his past. His future. A future that was, right now, slipping away. A future that held this compassionate and wonderful and loving woman, and the family that marriage to her would create—husband, wife and little girl. And then babies. Lots of babies.

He knew he would walk through hell for Caprice Kincaid. That was a hard, inescapable fact. So if he would walk through hell for her, why in the name of all that was holy would he let a few dollars keep them apart?

To do that, he'd have to be crazy. And crazy he was not.

He chased her and grabbed her before she'd gone five steps. He whirled her around to face him. Her face was pale. Her eyes shone like moonlight on gray waters.

He thought he'd never seen her more beautiful.

His love for her welled up inside him, and he tightened his grip on her arms.

"I'm up to it." His voice was forceful, rasping. And it rang with confidence. "I *am* up to it, dammit."

And that's when she crumpled. That's when the tears finally fell. And that's when he realized that her airy self-assurance had been a front.

"Oh, Gabe." Her voice caught in a sob. "I was so afraid. So afraid you would let me go…"

"Ah, sweetheart." Throat aching, body trembling, he brushed her tears away and wrapped his arms around her, as he'd been longing to do from the moment she returned. "Don't cry. Everything's going to be all right, I promise."

He kissed her then, and it was a kiss that made him feel as if he were floating to heaven. But heaven wasn't someplace in the distant skies; it was here in her arms.

After a long, long time, they finally drew apart. Not because they were ready to—they were nowhere near ready to—but because they both heard Willow's voice come from the doorway. Together, they turned to face her.

"Hi, Mrs. Kincaid." His daughter's endearingly mismatched eyes were fixed on Caprice. "Did it turn out all right?"

Gabe blinked. "Did what turn out all right?"

Willow fiddled with her hair. "It's a secret, Dad." Her eyes were still on Caprice.

Caprice crossed the kitchen, crouched and gave Willow a hug. "Yes, sweetie." She smiled. "Everything has turned out *perfectly* all right."

Willow yawned. "So you're staying forever?"

"Yes."

His daughter wound her arms around Caprice's neck and kissed her cheek. "That's good." She yawned again. "I tried to keep awake till you came, but I fell asleep."

"I'm sorry, Willow. My car had a flat. And I didn't want to call you in case your dad answered the phone."

"Willow, you knew Mrs. Kincaid was coming back?" Gabe scratched a puzzled hand through his hair.

"She called me when you were on your way back from Chicago. She said she had things to do but she'd be here by tonight—she wanted to get back to the lodge before the skiing season started so you wouldn't be too busy."

"Well, I'll be..." Gabe pretended to be aggrieved. "How come you didn't tell me all of this?"

"'Cause we like keeping secrets, don't we, Mrs. Kincaid!"

"Yes." Caprice gave her another hug. "We do."

Willow yawned again, and her eyelids started to shut.

"Young lady," Gabe said, "it's time you were back in bed. Besides," he added, "Mrs. Kincaid and I have a lot of talking to do."

Willow gave a drowsy giggle as he swept her into his arms. "A lot of *kissing,* you mean!"

"That, too, Miss Smarty-pants! Now say goodnight."

"Good night, Mrs. Kincaid."

"Good night, sweetie." Caprice gave her a final peck on the cheek then Gabe carried her from the room.

When he came back, he said with a lazy smile, "So, Mrs. Soon-To-Be-Ryland, where were we?"

She walked into his arms. "I don't know about you," she murmured, her eyes glowing at him with tender love, "but I was right here!"

"Are you aware," he teased, "that you have a smudge of what looks like *oil* on your brow?"

"I have? Oh, drat, I didn't want to look as messy when I got here as I did that first time. I thought I'd wiped it all off at the gas station. I tried to change the flat tire myself," she explained. "But I didn't get very far!"

He chuckled. "City girls." He shook his head. "They can't do squat!"

She fluttered her eyelashes provocatively. "You're sure about that?"

"Care to prove me wrong?"

She looped her arms around his neck and gave a husky laugh. "That, my darling Gabe, is going to be a pleasure!"

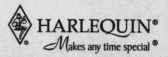

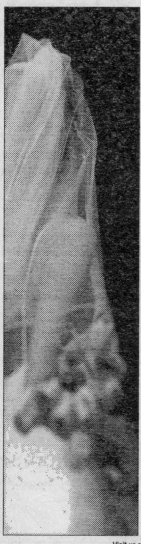